The Viscount's Mishap

The Trouble With Brothers: Book One

Linda Kaye

This book can only be dedicated to my own brother, Bob.

Dear Readers,

The trouble with brothers is that they are singlehandedly the most stubborn, annoying, protective, and yet loving creatures that the Good Lord ever saw fit to create. They insist that there are a separate set of rules for their behavior than for their sisters – especially their younger sisters. And while they mean well, they truly do try our patience at every turn.

Perhaps they were created to prepare us for our roles in later life – a colicky baby, an annoying in-law, a stubborn husband. The endless arguments defending what we feel are our basic rights are often met with a blank look that attempts to insult our intelligence.

Despite the trials and tribulations, a sister must endure with a brother, one thing is certain, after the dust settles, we wouldn't have them any other way.

Linda Kaye

Book Title Copyright © 2018 by Linda Kaye. All Rights Reserved.

All rights reserved. No part of this book may be reproduced in any form or by any electronic or mechanical means including information storage and retrieval systems, without permission in writing from the author. The only exception is by a reviewer, who may quote short excerpts in a review.

Cover designed by Kiselev Andrey Valerevich

This book is a work of fiction. Names, characters, places, and incidents either are products of the author's imagination or are used fictitiously. Any resemblance to actual persons, living or dead, events, or locales is entirely coincidental.

Linda Kaye
Visit my website at www.lindakayebooks.com

Printed in the United States of America

First Printing: Jul 2018

ISBN- 9781983397806

Contents

Chapter One 1
Chapter Two 18
Chapter Three 30
Chapter Four 37
Chapter Five 48
Chapter Six 62
Chapter Seven 72
Chapter Eight 83
Chapter Nine 91
Chapter Ten 102
Chapter Eleven 111
The Duke's Mistake 119
About The Author 120

Chapter One

Isabelle stepped outside and quickly moved into the shadows of the home so that nobody in the ball would notice her departure. Hugging the wall, she made her way all the way down to the other end, safe from the light and any prying eyes. She sighed, leaned back against the house and closed her eyes. She felt so much better out here. This was her first venture into society, and she hated being on display this way but at least she had her mask to hide her identity.

"What are you doing all the way out here alone?" a husky voice sounded.

Isabelle's eyes flew open. She looked around, but didn't see anybody. Then she heard him again. "Come here you sweet little thing. I bet your mother doesn't know you've made it all the way outside." She stiffened and strained her eyes looking into the gardens to find the voice. "Oh, now you want to give me kisses," the husky voice chuckled. "That's alright. I happen to love your kisses, sweetheart."

Isabelle realized that the voice was moving closer to her, and panic started to set in. She didn't want to be caught spying on two lovers who had met for a tryst in the garden.

"Let's get you to bed, darling."

Before Isabelle could move, the man started up the steps just feet from her. She gasped and his eyes flew up to eyes. Dear Lord, it was the duke of Kettering! A movement in his arms caught her attention. That's when she noticed the tiny white puppy squirming against his neck. Isabelle giggled at her mistake, but quickly covered her mouth to keep from insulting him.

He raised his chin in the most ducally manner, and she fought the urge to not laugh again. "What are you doing all the way out here alone?" he asked.

Isabelle chuckled. "Is that your standard line for ladies of all species?"

James Paget's eyes narrowed for a second and then he realized what she meant. His deep laughter joined hers. He grinned at her, "Is it working?"

"Well, I have no intention of giving you kisses, if that's what you mean?" she answered flatly but with a teasing grin.

He raised an eyebrow at her. "You might enjoy it," he tempted.

She sighed. "I'm sure I would enjoy it immensely; however, I have no desire to be caught outside with a man and be forced into a life sentence for one tiny error in judgement."

"Some would think I am quite a catch," he countered.

"And some feel the same about me, your grace."

He stiffened. "You know me?" When Isabelle nodded, he leaned closer to examine her face beneath the mask. "Then you have me at a disadvantage. Who might you be?"

"Somebody you won't see after tonight for quite a while." Even though she smiled, her tone sounded dejected.

"Giving up on the season already?" he asked as he took a step closer.

Isabelle shook her head. "I can't give up something I never wanted in the first place."

He cocked his head. "I thought young ladies dreamed of finding a husband and all that? Isn't that the point of a season?"

She sighed. "I didn't think you would understand either."

"Either?" he asked with a concerned tone.

She smiled weakly. "My family. They expect me to marry, and they can't seem to understand my apprehension."

Her gaze dropped to the ground. Her family would be so disappointed if they knew how she felt.

James had two options. He could walk away, which was probably the wisest so he wouldn't risk being caught alone with her, or he could risk it and talk with her. "Would you care to sit?" he nodded toward the bench against the house.

Isabelle looked at the duke for a few uncomfortable moments. James felt as if she could actual read his thoughts, and it was quite unsettling. She was a stunning lady but there was something about her demeanor that drew him to her, something he had never experienced before with another woman. When she sat primly on the bench, he found himself quite pleased to be able to spend a few more minutes with her.

"You don't want to marry or you aren't ready to marry?" he asked.

She smiled at him. "Oh, I do want to marry someday but just not now. And I would like to marry on my terms."

He cocked an eyebrow at her. "Your terms?"

"Do you have any idea what it is like to be looked at as if you are a fat purse or a prized mare? Not a single male has ever complimented me for anything other than my appearance and when they discover who I am, I can see their eyes light up. 'Beautiful *and* wealthy' they whisper behind my back. But I am so much more than that." She looked at his eyes wide with what she perceived as confusion. "You wouldn't understand."

He chuckled. "Since you know who I am, you must realize that your opinion couldn't be farther from the truth. I enter a ballroom and immediately I hear 'The duke is here!' Never my name, just my title."

Isabelle blushed slightly at her foolishness. "I'm sorry. I guess you would know better than anybody. Is that why you are hiding out here?"

"Not completely. I came outside, so I wouldn't have to watch my sister and my friend together. I am being told that they are a handsome couple and very well suited. And I don't like it one bit."

"Your sister is very kind. And she did seem very happy when I noticed her dancing earlier with Lord Southerby."

James rolled his eyes. "You're not helping me enjoy my sulking." He hugged the puppy closer to his chest. "At least you know how to make me feel better," he whispered against the soft fur.

"The puppy is making you feel better?" she mused.

Holding the wiggling animal up in front of him he smiled at the whimpering puppy. "A puppy always makes things better," he stated firmly. "Care to try?" He grinned temptingly at the lady.

Isabelle couldn't hold back at his charming behavior. She reached for the little puppy and held it close to her chest. The puppy nuzzled her neck and cuddled its soft and furry little body against her. When Isabelle heard the tiny animal sigh its contentment, she chuckled.

"You're feeling better already, aren't you?" James asked.

She had to admit, her worries seemed much smaller than they had just minutes before. She laid her cheek against the soft warm body snuggled to her neck. "I must confess, I do feel less concerned with my troubles."

James studied her and smiled at her enjoyment of the puppy. "Would you like to have this one? I can arrange it. After all, she belongs to my aunt who dotes on me." He grinned like a mischievous boy charming his way out of trouble.

Isabelle laughed. "Oh, would that I could, but it would be highly inappropriate for me to accept such a gift from you."

"No one needs to know where she came from. I can send her around to your home with a note. 'from a secret admirer'. That would start a few tongues wagging!"

"That is very kind of you, but alas, my father does not believe in house pets. He says an animal must earn its keep and a house pet is nothing more than an overgrown rodent," she sighed and pulled the sleeping puppy away from her body to return him. "But I am grateful that you have shared your secret to sanity with me. I promise I won't tell a soul."

Her face was turned toward his. James instinctively moved his head closer to her. His hand reached out to cup her cheek tenderly. His lips curved into a seductive smile. "You have made my evening a most pleasant one. I will never forget you, Lady Mysterious," he whispered just before he covered her soft lips with his hungry mouth.

The jolt that filled him shocked his senses. His tongue traced along her beautiful lips, beckoning her, tempting her to match him half way. He knew almost immediately that she was a complete innocent and the thought intoxicated him. He wanted to give her the most perfect first kiss. Enough to get her to confess her identity but not enough to frighten her. Little by little he coaxed her to open to him and offer her sweet tongue.

Isabelle was suddenly very warm. The duke's kisses were weakening her resolve to remain in the shadows, and she knew she could very easily throw caution to the wind. When his tongue snaked between her two lips to dance with her own, she surprised herself by relishing the feeling and she gasped.

Her gasp brought him back to reality, reminding that she was an innocent despite her mature behavior. He hoped his kiss would tempt her into revealing her name. Instead he found himself swimming in a desire that could only be quenched by one thing. Yet he knew it would destroy her spirit if he were to push his goal further. Regretfully he lifted his head.

Her hand innocently flew to her lips, her eyes wide with wonderment. He thought she looked adorable. "Please, tell me your name," he begged softly. "I've trusted you with my secret, trust me with yours."

She lowered her head. "I'm sorry, but I cannot," she admitted. "But I shall never forget this evening, your grace."

"James," he whispered. "Call me James." He surprised himself with the request. Only his closest friends and his mother called him by his given name. Even the ladies he dallied with called him your grace or Kettering. It was something he permitted only to his most intimate circle. "Will I see you again?" He chuckled sourly and wiped a large hand over his face. "I won't even know you if I do."

She placed her hand alongside his handsome face. "Time will tell," she paused and then added slowly, "James." She leaned in and gave him a tender kiss on his lips before pulling away. She stood and straightened her skirts. "Good evening, your grace. I've never enjoyed a more pleasant evening with such wonderful company."

He watched her walk away and felt as if she were taking a small piece of his soul with her. She was such a breath of fresh air, and he would have to meet her when her face was hidden behind a mask. But that was also part of the allure of a masked ball.

Anna Ashworth found her friend, Julia Paget, in the crowded ballroom. It wasn't an easy task with all the costumes and masks, but the two already knew what the other would be wearing so it was just a matter of locating the correct outfit. She began to pick her way across the edge of the floor to the refreshment table where Julia stood conversing with a tall pirate. Anna smiled, knowing that the pirate could be none other than Julia's fiancé, Kit Ashworth, Marquess of Southerby, and also known as Anna's brother.

Concentrating on her destination, Anna was startled when a gentleman bumped into her. She gasped and tried to regain her balance when he reached out to steady her. The second his glove contacted her wrist, she felt a charge rush through her. Looking up at the masked man, she melted at his coffee warm brown eyes. She smiled and was thrilled when he returned the gesture.

"Your majesty," he said with a nod to her Queen Guinevere costume. He bowed low and waited for her response.

Anna giggled. "Rise, Sir Lancelot," she directed.

The masked man rose and towered over her. "My fair queen, it must be fate. Would you do me the honor of granting me this dance?"

"It is I who would be honored," she flirted back. Under normal circumstances, Anna would have never agreed to a dance with a perfect stranger, but this was a masked ball. The unspoken purpose of a masked event was to step a toe just outside the bonds of propriety. To test society's rules without causing scandal. It was the thrill of being anonymous for one evening.

Her costume was a simple thin silk gown of the medieval style. The period style was not fashioned to cover her heavy underclothes and when she dressed this evening, she had wickedly decided to leave off her underclothes so the gown would lay against her properly. Scandalous for today's society, but quite acceptable for Guinevere's day. And just the thought of being so bare beneath the gown emboldened Anna's normally proper behavior.

Lancelot led her to the dance floor and held her just a bit closer than he should. But as with the true Lancelot, who cared not for the scandal of affair with his queen, this Lancelot cared not for what society thought of his actions. Parker Albany, Viscount Morely, hated social events and avoided them like the plague. However, a masked event was an opportunity to charm a soft, willing lady into his bed for the evening and was a welcome change to the bar maids, actresses, and ladies of questionable reputation that he usually enjoyed. If he played his cards right, this lovely piece gliding across the floor in his arms would fit right into his plans for the night.

"I am certainly the luckiest of men this evening," he commented with a warm and dangerous smile.

Anna returned the smile. "And why is that?"

Parker's fingers lightly squeezed her waist, offering a hint at what else he had to propose for the night. "You are by far the most enchanting, the loveliest lady present tonight. And here you are, in my arms."

"Well," she teased, "I am a queen after all. I should think that gives me an advantage over the mere peasant ladies around us."

Her partner raised an eyebrow. "Very true, your majesty. I can only wonder at what other advantages you might possess."

Anna was not skilled at flirtatious encounters but the words seemed to flow off her tongue as if she behaved so every day. "Well, I am told that only Sir Lancelot was able to unlock the deep secrets of his queen's desires."

A slow smile spread over Parker's masked face. "Then that is a challenge I cannot refuse."

Once the dance was over, Parker skillfully pulled the beautiful woman into an empty room. Finally, he had her alone, and he meant to sample every inch of her delightful offerings. He wasn't sure who she was, but with the ease at which she had followed him into this room, he knew she was experienced with these clandestine meetings. He kicked the door shut and reached behind him to lock it.

Pulling her into his arms, he smiled as she giggled. "I've finally got you alone. Can we get rid of these masks?" He reached for hers.

"But it's not midnight!" she gasped and held her hands protectively to her mask. "The rules, you know." There was a hint of daring in her tone, and Parker liked the idea of having an affair this way.

"Her majesty has a naughty side?" he murmured while nuzzling her neck. "I find that to my liking."

She turned her head towards him and his lips covered her own. He immediately plundered her inviting sweet mouth with his hot tongue, tasting and exploring until she was clinging to him, pulling him deeper and exploring his own mouth. He moaned. God, she was passionate.

Parker bent down to scoop her in his arms and carried her to a chaise. He laid her down and stretched out beside her. As his lips settled back on hers, his hand quickly lowered the bodice of her simple costume gown revealing her breasts. She brought her hand up to his hair as if his actions were normal and welcome, further cementing his thoughts that she knew what she was doing.

Anna knew this was wrong but she was so enthralled in the moment, the night, and this mysterious man making her feel ways that she had never known existed. His kisses sent a rush of heat to the very core of her being and she wanted to experience more of this sensation. His hand was on her breast, and she was letting him as if it were the most normal thing to happen!

Parker rolled her pert nipple between his thumb and forefinger, delighting in how erect it was. He had to taste her there. He lifted his mouth from her lips and trailed his tongue along the slender length of her neck. He left tiny kisses and nips along the way, lower and lower until his mouth captured her peak.

She sighed as his tongue swirled the point of her breast, playfully torturing her senses. Just when she thought she would die of pleasure, his mouth started to suckle her while his hands caressed both breasts. Her body arched upward to meet his tantalizing mouth. He continued to worry one breast for several enjoyable minutes before lifting his head. A small cry of disappointment slipped from her lips. He chuckled as he moved to the other breast and continued his assault on the second mound.

Anna was floating in desire. His hands were everywhere, sliding up the length of her legs, caressing her flat stomach, brushing against her long arms. He slid her gown up the length of her legs and Anna didn't resist when he lifted her bottom and pushed the thin material above her waist. When his hand rested on her thigh briefly, she heard his sharp intake of breath.

Parker smiled when he recovered from his shock of her wearing nothing under her gown. "You were looking for an adventure tonight," he murmured between kisses. "God, that excites me." He felt his manhood grow even harder than he could imagine at the thought. He sat up and removed his shirt and pulled off his boots. "Can we take the masks off now?"

She giggled. "Is it midnight yet?"

He shook his head and chuckled softly. "Then I shall have to make do with your rules, Your Majesty." He pulled her into a sitting position and pulled the gown over her body but stopping as it hung around her neck. "Hold your mask or you risk breaking your own rules," he teased. When she did, he slipped it over her head and tossed it aside.

He laid her back against the chaise and admired her flawless body. "You are so beautiful," he whispered. "I have to taste all of you." He knelt on the floor before her and stroked her body with his large powerful hands. He took one perfect ankle in his hand and lifted it over his bare shoulder. Turning his head, he gently kissed the inner thigh of that leg before doing the same with the other leg.

Anna's breathing came faster, a mixture of anticipation and fear. He was so close to her most intimate place that she didn't know how to react. This was madness and she knew she should quickly end it, but just as she was about stop him, his tongue reached out and caressed her in the most indecent way. Anna gasped and fell back against the pillow. Oh, this was most certainly a sin. Nothing but pure sin could feel this wonderful, but heaven help her, she could not stop him now if she wanted.

Parker held her tightly against his mouth as he licked, lapped, tasted, probed, and savored this most delightful place. She rocked against him and he increased his intensity. Her soft whimpers were music to his ears as she neared her pleasured. Wanting to give her more without giving up his enjoyment at the moment, he slid a digit inside her.

"Oh, my God," she cried in a barely audible murmur. She knew something was happening to her that could only bring more enjoyment than she was already experiencing. Her hips moved in rhythm against his mouth's assault. She no longer cared that this encounter had gone way beyond an adventure. All she was concerned with was finding out what was building so deep inside her that when the dam finally broke, she nearly screamed her relief.

Even as she found her pleasure, Parker continued to lash her with his tongue, prolonging her enjoyment and his as well. When she finally began to tremble at his touch, he reluctantly lifted his head and tenderly kissed each inner thigh. "You liked that?" he teased.

Anna blushed even though she gave him a sweet smile. She watched him stand and unfasten his breeches. This was where she must stop him! She couldn't allow a perfect stranger such liberties. What was she thinking! As the garment was shoved down past his hips and his manhood sprang forth, she gasped in fascination. Her hand reached out tentatively to touch him. As her hand closed around him, he hissed and she let go, fearful that she had done something wrong.

"If I let you do that, I'm afraid I won't last long, love," he teased.

She was grateful for his words as it reminded her this had to stop. She began to sit up, but he assumed she was reaching for a kiss which he happily obliged. Long, sensuous, full of promises of more. She moaned softly and did not realize he had nestled himself between her legs.

Parker's member was resting just at the edge of her hot opening, ready to surge onward. But Parker was going to ride this kiss for all it was worth. He had never been so intoxicated by a woman in his life. Suddenly there was a loud roar from beyond the door.

Anna snapped out of her fantasy and raised her head. "What is that?" she asked.

"Midnight," he replied as his lips found her breasts once more. "Time for the unmasking, Your Majesty. And a perfect time for it."

Anna reached up and shyly pulled her mask off. "Yours too," she whispered down at him as he was paying careful attention to her breasts. His raised one hand and pulled his off. Tearing himself away from his newest obsession, he lifted his head to gaze upon the face of the lady who was so passionate and alluring. And then their eyes met.

"Oh my God!" Parker cried and sat up immediately. "You! What in the hell do you think you are doing?"

Anna nearly fainted when she realized her mystery man was her own brother's friend, Parker Albany, Viscount Morely. She tried to cover her nakedness with her hands and felt her face turn bright red.

Parker threw his head back and laughed an evil sound. "Don't act shy now. My God! Do you have any idea what we just about did? What we already have done?" He turned away and ran his fingers through his hair. Suddenly he stopped and faced her. "You let me…" He looked down at the apex of her legs but couldn't even find the words to finish the sentence.

Tears started streaming down her cheeks and she shook from the anger in his words. She knew she should be ashamed, but hearing him describe her disgraceful behavior was more than she could take.

"Stop crying and get dressed," he snapped and tossed her gown at her. He quickly pulled his own costume back on. She pulled her gown over her head and stood trying to smooth it out. Once they were both fully dressed and their masks back in place, he grabbed her arm and pulled her towards the door. "Let's go."

"Where?" she asked dazed at his abrupt behavior.

"To find your brother," he hissed. "And I hope I only end up shackled to you instead of waiting for him to kill me in a duel. Although at this point, I'm not sure which would be worse." He heard the cruelty in his own words, but he was so angry right now that he couldn't think straight.

"No!" she cried and stopped. "Please, you can't tell Kit. I would be mortified."

Parker loomed down over her and clutched her chin in his hand forcing her to look at him. "Lady Anna, I have just spent the better part of a quarter hour with my tongue buried inside you in the most intimate of ways. You should be mortified."

A fresh round of silent tears fell and Parker could feel her tremble in fright at his touch. So different from just a few moments ago when they both relished the pleasure of the other's touch. An image of his own sister filled his mind, and he knew that he would kill any man who talked to her the way he had just talked to Anna. He released her chin and took a step back trying to calm himself. Trying to take in what had just happened and with who. He ran his hand over his face again as he thought of a plan.

Anna took that moment to flee the room, pushing him away and causing Parker to lose his balance. She rushed back into the ballroom and scurried as fast as she could go. She slowed when she was back in view of the others and headed straight to the entrance where a footman quickly opened the door and escorted her outside to her coach.

She sat back and tried to steady her breathing. Parker Albany! How could she have behaved so! She was horrified at how foolish she had been. And worse, if Parker told Kit, her brother would never look at her the same again. He would be so disappointed and hurt with her behavior. She closed her eyes and prayed Parker would not say a word. After the short ride home, she sent the coach back for her brother's use and a message that she had become tired and returned home early.

Parker Albany had regained his footing and tried to catch up to Lady Anna, but the crowd refused to part for him. By the time he made his way outside, he could only watch the Southerby carriage drive away, growing smaller and smaller. "Dammit!" he swore. He tore the mask off his face and launched it as far as he could send it through the air.

"Problem?" a voice asked in the darkness.

Parker spun towards the voice and saw his friend Jack Cavanaugh, the duke of Brighton, standing off to one side of the entrance partially hidden in the shadows. "Have you taken to lurking in the bushes now?"

Jack laughed and stepped into the lamp light glowing from the street. "I never lurk. I'm just waiting to give a lady a ride home."

Parker snorted. "I bet you are." He knew Jack very well. "And who is the damsel in distress?"

A broad smile crossed the devilishly handsome duke's face. "Mary Tatum."

A vision of the beautiful blonde countess came to Parker's mind, and even he was impressed. "Marsh will kill you," he commented mentioning the woman's husband.

"Nonsense," he replied.

"You live for the thrill of it, don't you?"

"Don't you?" Jack smiled back. "Who just chased a young lady out of the house, her running away in tears?"

Parker's head shot up. His gaze narrowed intently at his friend. "She was still crying?"

Jack raised one eyebrow. "Who was she?"

A heavy sigh filled the air. "A horrible, horrible mistake."

Jack chuckled. "She looked anything but horrible to me. Did the great Parker Albany disappoint a lady to tears? Are you losing your touch?"

"I don't want to discuss her," Parker said through clinched teeth.

"Very well," Jack answered. "Let's go to the club and have a drink."

"What about your countess?"

Jack shrugged. "There's a willing woman just around the next corner. Will do the chit good to know I had better things to do tonight." He threw an arm around Parker and led him towards his carriage.

Chapter Two

Yeats opened the door open for his employer. "Good morning, my lord," he said in a low voice. Nothing in his expression or tone indicated the viscount's disheveled appearance. His cravat hanging loose, his shirt untucked and wrinkled, his hair uncombed, and he smelled of whiskey and cheap perfume.

Parker blinked and swayed trying to keep his balance. He didn't argue when Yeats took his arm and helped him upstairs to his rooms.

"Shall I order a bath for you, my lord?" the butler asked.

Parker fell backwards onto his bed with a groan. Yeats sighed and bent down to remove his boots. Once that was completed, he did his best to tug and pull the six-foot one-inch man up on his bed and wrestle his unconscious form out of his jacket.

"I take it you would rather wait for your bath," he mumbled. Parker's soft snores gave him the answer he was expecting. He shook his head and left the room to inform Parker's valet that he was resting.

At the same time, Anna was pushing around her breakfast on her plate with her fork. She had slept very little reliving the events of last night over and over in her mind. She would never forget the feelings and sensations Parker had opened her horizons to, but she was haunted by the humiliation of allowing him such liberties. It was a sobering realization that she had been drawn into such a dangerous game, but then to discover that it was Parker, of all people!

Parker Albany. Tall, blonde, brown eyes, well-built, graceful. The list could go on and on. But she could also add rake, debaucher, sinful, reckless, and a hell-raiser. She should know his faults, as they were the same faults her brother possessed even though she loved her brother dearly. At least those were Kit's faults until he had set his sights on her friend Julia. Now he was so clearly smitten and in love, she wondered how he could ever have lived such a wild life beforehand.

"You're very quiet today," he brother stated from the end of the table.

Anna's head snapped up at his words and she stared at him for a moment. She wondered for a moment if she had spoken her thoughts aloud.

Kit frowned at her. "Are you sure you aren't ill? I would never imagine you would leave your first masked ball early and you couldn't even bother to tell me first."

It was a clear statement that her brother was not pleased with her choice, and Anna knew that he would be angry. But her only thought at that moment was to escape Parker, and his cruel, hurtful words that still rang through her head. When Kit returned home last night, he had gone straight to her room to check on her. Anna had been terrified.

Despite being wild and a despoiler of women, Kit was a devoted brother. Intent on keeping his little sister protected from anything hurtful or unkind. She was perfect, graceful, and in his eyes, a complete innocent. And for the most part, she was all that until last night. That's why she had begged Parker not to say a word to him. She would die if Kit ever thought less of her.

She sighed. "I'm sorry. I didn't want to ruin the evening for Julia and you. And I'm not ill. I just grew a bit warm and the crowd just seemed so large. I needed to get away. And I did have a footman escort me to the carriage."

"Still, I don't like that you wouldn't come to me or send word. You should know better than to leave alone. I don't want that to happen again." His tone implied that he had spoken and she was not to argue with him.

Anna sighed again and pushed away from the table. She stood and walked over to Kit's chair and kissed his cheek. "I'm sorry. And you are right. I should know better. I love you."

Kit's stern face softened and he hugged her while kissing the top of her head. "I love you, too, you little muttonhead. I just worry about you. It was much easier before you grew up."

Anna chuckled. "It's good for you to be on your toes now and then. You've grown too accustomed to everything falling into place as you wish."

He snorted. "Oh, little sister, if only my life were that charmed."

Anna smiled sweetly at him. She knew he was thinking of their father passing away unexpectedly and Kit suddenly finding himself responsible for his mother and sister. Their mother had elected to stay at their country estate, never quite getting over the heartache of losing her husband until her heart just gave out one night leaving Anna with only her brother.

"I think I'm going to rest a bit. I'm not used to such late hours," she stated.

"Late? I hate to inform you, but you left hours earlier than you would normally be expected to remain in attendance. But go rest. I'm sure it was exhausting for you regardless."

Three hours later, Anna was awakened by her door bursting open. She opened her eyes to find Julia standing over her. And then to her horror, she saw their friend Isabelle, Parker's sister, standing beside Julia.

"Let's have it," Julia demanded with her hands on her hips.

Anna pretended ignorance. "What do you mean?"

Julia sat down on the bed and Anna was forced to slide over and give her room. "Don't play games with me. You disappeared for quite a while and it was so strange that Sir Lancelot also disappeared at the same time."

Anna sucked in a breath. Could Isabelle know how her brother was dressed? She tried to give Julia a pleading look to end this line of questioning.

"Sir Lancelot?" Isabelle asked. "My, that sounds romantic. Guinevere and Lancelot? And tell me, fair Guinevere, did you have an illicit affair with your king's knight?" She giggled.

Anna studied her for a moment, trying to decipher if she knew Lancelot's true identity. "It wasn't that illicit," she finally admitted.

"Ooohh!" Julia squealed. "And what does that mean? Did he kiss you?" She was giggling and bouncing on the bed. Anna's blush told her the truth. "Oh, he did! And was it wonderful?"

"It was interesting," Anna said softly.

"Interesting?" Isabelle inquired. "That's an interesting way to describe it. Was it not exciting? Did he not steal your breath away? Did his touch leave you begging for more of something you couldn't quite understand?"

Both friends turned to stare at Isabelle's descriptive words. She was the kindest and friendliest of their set of friends, yet her choice of attire and heavy makeup rarely caused a person to give her a second glance.

"And how would you know of these feelings?" Julia demanded.

Isabelle looked innocently at them both. "I read," she replied. "But we aren't talking about me," she added shifting the attention back to Anna.

Anna suddenly had both friends staring at her, waiting for her to explain her answer. "It was everything you described and more," she admitted and let her mind drift back to the first kiss she had shared with Parker.

Julia clapped her hands together like a child. "Oh, I knew it! So, who was your mystery knight."

The color left her face, and she swallowed. "Sir Lancelot," she finally answered.

"You don't know his identity?" Isabelle asked in a shocked voice.

Anna shook her head. "But he doesn't know mine either," she quickly added.

"Well, perhaps your season will include trying to deduce who he was. A real-life mystery," Julia noted.

"And don't you dare tell my brother," Anna returned.

Julia's eyes widened. "I would never do that, and you know it."

"I know," Anna admitted. "But enough of me. Let's talk about your betrothal ball. Three nights from now. Are you excited?" She knew this topic would draw the attention away from her as Julia loved to talk of nothing else but her wedding.

Julia shrugged. "I think it's just a formality that James wants to force Kit to endure. As a matter of fact, he insisted on it despite my protesting that it wasn't necessary."

Isabelle laughed. "I think your brother wanted to see how much Southerby wants you as his wife. He can't be happy you are marrying one of his best friends."

Anna laughed. "And not just a friend, but one as wild and sinful as they come."

There were five close friends, Parker, James, Kit, Trey and Jack. Each one as handsome and dangerous as the next. And ironically, they each had a sister, Isabelle, Julia, Anna, Sophie, and Lucy that were all friends. And somehow, Kit had fallen in love with James' sister, Julia and all hell would have broken loose had Julia's mother not stepped in and reminded James who was really the head of the family. James had been forced to stand aside and watch his worst nightmare come true.

"That's not true!" Isabelle countered. "Not a one of them come close to Jack Cavanaugh's reputation."

"True. That particular duke is beyond all hopes," Anna admitted. "Kit says he won't be attending the ball."

Julia laughed. "He said he wouldn't be caught dead at a ball, but he would attend the wedding 'If James didn't kill Kit first'." She laughed harder. "Mother has threatened to publicly blister James' bare arse if he makes a scene at the ball or the wedding."

The three girls laughed and then began to discuss the finer details of the ball and the wedding plans. By the time luncheon was ready, Anna had almost forgotten about her humiliating behavior of the night before.

Three nights later, Parker dropped in a chair beside Jack at one of their clubs. Jack glanced at him and then to the clock on the wall before looking back at his cards. "Thought you had a betrothal ball to attend tonight," he noted dryly.

"I can't do it alone," he answered and motioned for a drink.

Jack laughed. "I sure as hell hope you don't expect me to escort you."

Parker glared at him. "Some friend you are." He downed his drink and raised his glance for another. "It wouldn't hurt you to go. Kit is your friend, too."

"Yes, and I've told him he's a damn fool for getting married. Besides, I planned on an early night, going to see Tessa. She's been whining and crying that I'm ignoring her." The handsome young duke frowned as he thought of his current mistress.

"You usually get rid of them when they start to dictate to you. Are you growing soft?" Parker teased.

Jack snorted. "Not at all. She just happens to be, shall we say, always grateful when I do visit her." He laughed as he thought of her talents. "But she is getting a bit tiresome."

Parker shook his head. "I heard Lowdes was attending tonight. Overheard him talking about meeting a certain countess."

Jack sat up, his eyes narrowed in anger. "My Mary?" he demanded in a low growl.

"Well, I think her husband would take exception to you calling her your Mary, but yes. That's the one."

"Like hell he's meeting her," Jack snapped. "Get up, let's go."

Parker smiled as he downed his drink and followed Jack out of the club. He already knew that Lowdes would have never been included on the guest list, but he also knew that was the only way to get Jack to go with him.

Jack Cavanaugh and Jason Havens, the earl of Lowdes, had been in constant competition with one another since their early school days. One was always trying to best the other in studies, sport, hunting, and now as grown men, with women.

Parker knew that Jack couldn't sit still and let Lowdes have a chance at a woman Jack was interested in. And knowing Jack's weakness ensured that Parker might have a chance to see the lady who had haunted his thoughts and dreams.

Kit was standing by his fiancé and sister watching the dancing when it happened. First a gasp, followed by whispers as the room turned to stare before the crowd parted in shock. Kit shook his head as his friends approached. "Damn, Jack, you sure do know how to make an entrance," he chuckled.

Jack shrugged and grinned. "Heard the party needed to be livened up a bit." This was one of the reasons he avoided society events. He hated the reaction.

Kit shook his hand and pulled him closer to clap his other hand on Jack's back. "Thank you for coming. It means a lot to me."

Jack felt a little awkward knowing that the only reason he had decided to come was because of a woman he wanted to bed. Fortunately, before he had to respond, Parker cleared his throat.

"And aren't you glad to see me as well?" Parker asked.

The group laughed and Kit shook his hand as well. "Jack, you know Lady Julia," Kit turned towards his sister and saw her face slightly flushed. He took a deep breath. "Anna, I want you to look at this face and memorize it," he nodded towards Jack, "and should you ever encounter him outside of my presence, you are to run away as fast as you can. Do you understand me?"

Anna's gaze shifted to her brother and smiled, but realized that he was somewhat serious. She looked back to the Duke of Brighton. "Your grace," she said softly and dipped a curtsy.

Jack bowed over her outstretched hand in such a smooth, charming manner. "Lady Anna," he drawled. "It is a pleasure to make your acquaintance."

Anna's heart fluttered just being so near to his presence. He was as handsome as the stories said. Midnight black hair, a bit too long to be fashionable, but tonight tied neatly in a que behind his neck. Sapphire blue eyes, his skin was darkened by the sun and set his white straight teeth off. She felt a chill run down her spine, and knew he was every bit as dangerous as the rumors claimed.

"I've heard much about you, from Lucy," he continued.

Lucy. Anna was suddenly snapped from her day dreaming and smiled. "Yes, Lucy is a dear friend. She mentioned she'll be making her bow later this season."

Kit and Parker laughed and Jack frowned, his lips held tightly together. "We'll see. I think she's too young, but mother says she outranks me on this decision."

Just then the orchestra started warming up and Kit looked at Julia. "Are you ready for this?"

She smiled back at him. "Of course."

Kit started to take her hand but then stopped and turned towards Anna. He glanced at Parker and Jack standing beside her. There was no way in hell he would ask Jack to keep her company while he and Julia danced. Parker was the lesser of the two evils but lately he had been as wild as Jack. Before he had to tell her to run along to the ladies retiring room and lock herself in there, his future brother in law, James approached.

"Kettering," he acknowledged. When James nodded, he added "Would you mind keeping my sister company for the opening set?"

James snorted. "You most certainly can trust me with your sister. Don't worry, I wouldn't do anything to your sister that you wouldn't do to mine." His tone was clipped and short, but his meaning well implied.

Kit's eyes flared and he took a step toward his future brother in law. But before he could respond, Lady Isabelle stepped between the two men. "Have no fear, my lord," she interrupted. "I have just come to abscond with Lady Anna so you won't need to worry about her."

Kit glanced down at Parker's sister and back at James. Julia pulled on his arm at that moment and he allowed himself to be led away.

"That was truly uncalled for, your grace," Isabelle chided James.

James grinned down at her. "But I made my point."

"Why don't you just stop being stubborn and admit that Lord Southerby deeply loves your sister? Is it some sense of arrogant pride that you men possess?"

Anna shook her head and grabbed Isabelle's arm. "Let's go and leave these boys to their games." The two friends linked arms and started to walk away.

The three men watched the duo fade into the crowd. James was distracted by an elderly guest, and Jack leaned close and whispered to Parker, "You crazy son of a bitch."

Parker's head snapped around and was met with Jack's devilish grin. "What?"

"Kit will rip your head off and shove it up your ass," he replied but still grinning like a well-fed cat.

"I have no idea what you're talking about," Parker snapped back in a low tone.

"What are you two whispering about?" James asked joining the conversation.

Jack smiled. "Just enjoying your set down by Lady Isabelle. Parker, you should be proud of your little sister's grit."

Parker frowned. "If only she'd allow Lady Julia or Lady Anna to assist her in dressing. That would improve her chances. At least I don't have to worry about her attracting the wrong sort. Sometimes I think I won't have to worry about her attracting any sort."

"I like Lady Isabelle," James spoke up. "She's more honest and forthright than most of the people in this room."

Jack smiled. "I like her, too. Any young lady that can tell off a duke publicly and walk away with her head high is aces in my book. Besides there is more there than meets the eye."

Parker shook his head. "I don't know." Parker loved his sister dearly and he dreaded the day when she actually started taking these events seriously only to discover she wasn't considered by most society men.

James chuckled. "Come on, you're starting to sound like Trey. Gloom and doom over his sister."

"And where is our fifth this evening?" Jack inquired.

James raised his head to the balcony above. "Watching and learning for when his sister makes her debut."

Jack laughed, causing heads to turn their way. "He's like a damn old woman. Worries too much about the girl."

Parker shook his head. "Come on. Trey's not had it easy. From what he says she's a bit on the bulky side and awkwardly shy. He's terrified her come out will be one thing he can't make right for her."

The men all knew that Trey Harrow, the Earl of Chelmsworth, had raised his sister alone since his parents were killed in a carriage accident when Trey was just sixteen and his sister, Sophronia, was only six. He wanted every aspect of her life to be perfect, and the closer her formal introduction to society neared, the more nervous he became. Sophronia had been staying with a spinster aunt for the past few years, so the men only had Trey's words to go on when it came to the girl's chances.

Jack sighed. "Well, gentlemen, I think I've shocked society enough for one evening. Time for me to crawl back into the shadows. Are you coming, Morely?" he asked of Parker.

Parker handed his empty glass to a passing servant and nodded. "Kettering?" he asked James, knowing that James could not and would not leave his sister's betrothal. When James just shook his head, the two men left.

Chapter Three

Jack wasted no time once he and Parker were back in the carriage. "Damn, Parker. Did you really fuck Kit's sister?"

Parker glared at him. "Jesus, Jack. Have you lost all sense of proper behavior in that depraved lifestyle you keep?"

Jack grinned. "I beg your pardon. Please tell me you didn't introduce Lady Anna to the world of Viscount Morely's seductive charms?"

"Why are you drawing this conclusion?" Parker tried to remain calm. It had been hard enough to be in the same room with Anna let alone be so close to her. He had ignored her on purpose, but he had also noticed that she hadn't once glanced his way.

Jack chuckled. "You forget. I saw her running from the ball that night. Even though she was wearing a mask, I never forget a female's body. And a very delectable piece it was."

Parker was suddenly on him, grabbing his coat and pulling Jack to his face. "Do not refer to her in that manner ever again," he growled. He let go of Jack with a shove and sat back down on his side staring out the window.

Jack straightened his coat and watched Parker's heavy breathing. "You did, didn't you?" he asked softly. "Hell, I was teasing before but I…"

"No," Parker interrupted. "I did not."

"But something happened," Jack noted. Silence. Parker said not a word. He continued to stare out the window and ignore Jack. Jack knew better than to push it.

Four hours and many rounds of brandy later, Parker's mood had turned from quiet to nearly pathetic. Jack half dragged, half carried his friend back to his carriage. He directed the driver to take them to Parker's home.

"What did happen?" he asked softly as they started moving.

Parker looked up at him with eyes so sad and ashamed. "I didn't know who she was. It was Lady Cordale's masked ball. I thought she was, well, you know. Looking for a tumble."

Jack waited for him to continue. He felt like a gossipy old woman just waiting for the juicy part to be told, but he also had realized by this time that whatever had happened was not good. When Parker didn't speak, Jack prodded for more. "Did she know who you were?"

"No," he answered quickly. "She was as surprised as I was when we took off our masks."

"Well, then you're worrying too much. You kissed her, took off your masks, and no harm done," Jack reasoned.

Parker shook his head. "Our masks were the last things we removed."

The carriage lurched to a halt. When the door opened, Jack leaned over and shut it quickly. "That last?" he repeated trying to get Parker's mind back on their conversation. "Are you saying there could be a future little viscount brewing? Dammit Parker, even I know you should already be leg shackled for that!"

Again, Parker shook his head. "No. It didn't get that far. But it was very close. Almost beyond close. If you had any idea what we did…" Parker took a deep breath and his face became angry. "What she allowed me to do to her…Well, her reputation would be destroyed beyond any redemption if it was ever known."

"Does Kit know?"

Parker snorted. "I'm still alive, so no, I don't think he has any clue."

Jack slapped his friend on the knee. "Well, don't beat yourself up. You taught her a few things she'll no doubt never forget. No permanent damage."

"You don't understand," Parker whined. "I called her everything imaginable when I realized who she was. Told her she should be ashamed of the way she had behaved. And even though it was all true, dear God, Jack. I hurt her plain and simple."

A low whistle crossed the duke's lips. "Apologize. Man up and tell her you are sorry for your behavior."

Parker wiped his face with his hands and let his head fall back against the seat. "I don't think that will solve all my problems."

The wedding of Julia Paget and Christopher Kit Ashworth, 6th Marquess of Southerby, was a small private affair as both parties did not want anything elaborate. They had included only their closest friends and family members on the guest list. Julia was beautiful and Kit was as dashing as ever. They made a perfect couple.

Anna smiled brightly at her brother's happiness as well as her friend's, too. She had tried to stay tucked in a corner, away from Parker's sight and his chastising gaze. She looked up once to see him watching her, but she quickly turned and walked away. It was bad enough that she had behaved so wantonly that night, but every time she saw him or heard his name, she was reminded of it all over again.

She shivered when she recalled the way he had touched her, the way he had made her feel. It was wonderful. Anna had never imaged a man could make her feel that way, and that made this fiasco all the much harder to take.

Her head told her that she was just another one of his conquests that men like him seemed to collect. At least she knew he wouldn't be bragging about it to his friends or else Kit would have killed him by now. And probably her as well.

Isabelle found her standing behind a large fern. "What on earth are you doing back here?" she asked.

Anna shook her head. "I just wanted to be alone for a bit."

"I understand," Isabelle answered. "It's sometimes nice to be alone. I'll come fetch you when mother and father are ready to leave." She hugged her friend. "We'll have so much fun for the next week. It will be just like having a sister."

Anna smiled but inside she panicked. It had been planned weeks ago that she would stay with Isabelle and her family for Kit's honeymoon week. Before her scandalous night with Parker. She would be trapped in his home, and if he stopped over she couldn't very well avoid him in front of his parents. So far he had done nothing but ignore her, and that was fine with Anna.

Parker knew exactly where Anna was, and knew why she was trying to conceal herself. Each time he glanced her way, she shifted her position. Once he had caught her eye, he knew she saw him, and she deliberately turned away. He needed to apologize to her, but he could never find the right moment.

He watched her talking to his sister behind her protective fern. She was beautiful tonight, but nowhere near as beautiful as she had been completely naked and open to him, his hands, his mouth. His manhood shifted, and Parker scolded himself. That was the last thought he should be having!

Parker couldn't get the girl out of his head. Everywhere he turned, he caught sight of somebody that reminded him of her. Even when he closed his eyes to sleep, all he could see was the most perfect female in all her glory as she had been that night.

He swallowed and moved his gaze past her. How much longer did he have to stay here to be polite. He needed to get away from her before he acted too rashly and drew attention. But leaving before the bride and groom would attract even more attention, so he stayed. And it was pure hell.

Anna had been fortunate during her stay with Isabelle's family that Parker had not visited, however on her final evening her luck ran out. She and Isabelle were descending the stairs to go into dinner when the front door opened.

"Good evening, my lord," Finley, the Albany's butler said warmly.

"Finley," a deep voice returned in kind.

Anna's head snapped up as she heard Parker's brief exchange with the butler. She froze as a smiling Parker turned around and faced the stairs. His gaze met hers and he was transfixed by her.

"Parker!" Isabelle cried and rushed down the stairs to greet him. She flung herself into his arms. "I didn't know you were joining us this evening."

"It's bad form when one ignores a direct request from the Countess," he teased referring to his mother. "But as usual, you have surprised me. I did not know I wasn't the only guest."

Isabelle looked back at Anna and grinned. "She's been staying with us while Kit and Julia enjoy a little time alone. Personally, I think she should stay longer. I've rather enjoyed having a sister this week."

Parker kissed his sister's cheek. "I never knew you were so disappointed in having a brother. Shall I convince our parents to try for a sister for us?"

Lord and Lady Tenworth, the parents in question, appeared just behind Isabelle on the stairs. "The answer is no," Trenton Albany stated loudly. "Get yourself a wife if you want Isabelle to have a sister."

Parker nearly choked at his words. "Sorry, sis," he grinned. "It appears you will have to live with just a brother then."

Anna knew that she had to move out of her hosts way, so she made her way down the remaining steps. She stepped to one side avoiding Parker's glance. The earl and his wife passed the threesome and headed toward the dining room.

"Shall we go in?" Parker asked and offered an arm to each lady.

Isabelle laughed and happily took her brother's arm, but Anna hesitated just a second. When Parker glanced down at her, Anna met him with a cold, steely stare. He swallowed and hoped she wouldn't cause a scene in his parents' home. Reluctantly she accepted his arm.

The atmosphere during the meal held a strained and tense feeling. Lord and Lady Trenton kept up light conversation and seemed not to notice anything out of the ordinary. Anna was unusually quiet, and Parker answered with the barest of words. It was Isabelle who realized something had changed in Anna with the appearance of her brother this evening.

She was used to being a wallflower in public, and she had always delighted in what she could learn while being ignored by the rest of society. She decided to put those skills to the test and see what she could learn.

Anna concentrated mostly on her food, only raising her gaze when a question was directed to her from her hosts. Parker looked almost hopeful each time Anna glanced up but his hope seemed to fade each time she avoided his direction. Isabelle hid a smile. There was something afoot here, and she was certain she would soon find out the truth.

Chapter Four

Two weeks later the Yates annual ball was in full swing. Isabelle turned her head away from her dance partner and softly tsked at what she happened to see. She shook her head and calmly returned her gaze to her partner. He was staring at her with one eyebrow cocked.

"Isn't it bad form to ignore your partner during a dance?" he asked.

Isabelle stared at him for just a brief second before a giggle burst forth. When James Paget, the Duke of Kettering, rolled his eyes at her response, she giggled even more. "On the contrary, Jamie," she answered in her haughtiest tone, "one can learn so much while dancing as you are given a full view of the others in attendance."

He grinned at her. "I never thought you to be a gossip, Izzy." She hated being called Izzy as much as he hated being called Jamie, but it was a private joke between the two.

Her brows furled together with her frown. "I am not a gossip," she clipped shortly. "I am merely observant, and I collect the information I observe. Gossips repeat. I observed."

James threw back his head in laughter, ignoring the sudden heads who turned their way. "And what have you observed that has you so interested?"

Isabelle pursed her lips together in thought for a moment. "Well, I can't reveal it or that would make me a gossip, but I will give you a hint."

"Go on."

"Observe my brother over there," she said softly. "No! Don't turn and look at him now. Wait until he is over my shoulder." She smiled sweetly up at him. "Now observe what he is observing himself."

"He's looking at...Oh!" he gasped. Parker was staring at Kit's sister Anna with such heated intensity James thought the poor girl didn't stand a chance. He glanced down at Isabelle only to be met with a broad knowing smile.

"See, I'm observant, not a gossip," she gloated. He turned his head again and she cleared her throat making him look back her way again.

"Kit will kill him," he said under his breath.

"Not necessarily. Did you kill Kit?" she asked impishly.

James rolled his eyes again and sighed. He wasn't happy that his best friend had married his little sister, but even he had to admit Kit loved Julia with all his heart. "Did you know this?"

She shook her head. "I suspected, but I didn't have any proof until tonight. Well, that's not completely true, but I can't reveal all of my secrets." They turned again in the dance and Isabelle caught sight of something else. "Oh, no." Her face fell and turned to anger.

"What's wrong? Has our lovesick fool been caught?" James teased.

"I need some lemonade or just, I need to..."

James quickly led her to the side of the room. "Are you alright? Would you like me to get your mother?"

She shook her head. "No, I'm just angry. Let's get a good view for the rest of this show."

"Show?" he asked as he followed her along the edge of the floor until she stopped. "What's going on?"

Isabelle sighed. "You've noticed who Parker is staring at, but who is watching Parker?"

James scanned the room, thinking that Parker was being watched by another ardent suitor, but he saw nothing out of the ordinary. He shook his head, and then made another sweep of the faces. This time he noticed something. "Who is that?" he whispered to Isabelle.

"That is Marlena Barnes, first rate trouble maker," she hissed.

"I take it she's not a friend of yours?" he teased. He watched the young lady across the way stare at his friend. Then her glance moved to Anna and her expression changed to anger. Could this lady be upset with the competition? A smirk crossed the girl's face as she glanced back at Parker. "And what is she about?"

Isabelle sighed again. "She's not interested in Parker, if that is what you mean. She is interested in making sure Parker's interest is directed away from Anna and placed on her."

"Why would she do that if she's not interested in him herself?" James was confused at the workings of the female mind.

"Look at her. Tell me what you see at first glance. Forget anything else I have said."

James coyly slid another glance towards the girl in question. She was breath-taking on first sight. Blonde hair, blue eyes. Her pale pink gown shimmered in the candlelight. Her bodice was cut much lower than the other debutantes revealing an extremely well-built bosom. Innocence and seduction all in the same breath, he noted.

"She is beautiful," Isabelle admitted with a tone of defeat.

"But?" James inquired knowing that there was more to this Marlena's countenance than met the eye.

She exhaled. "Well, my mother always says that beauty is in the eye of the beholder."

"Meaning she's a nasty piece of work under the pretty wrappings?" James chuckled.

Isabelle playfully slapped his arm in a scold. "Sshhh! And actually she can be a very nice person."

"And what are you two up to now?" a new voice inquired from behind them. They turned to find James' sister, Julia giving them her best motherly stare.

Julia was not surprised to find Isabelle and James together, plotting and whispering as usual. They both seemed to hover together at these events providing a sense of protection from the match makers who thought their daughters would be perfect as James' duchess or whose sons were quite thin in the pockets and needed the large dowry that came with Lady Isabelle.

"Where's Kit?" Isabelle asked quickly.

"Oh, he's back there," she turned to indicate her husband but found herself pulled in front of James and Isabelle. "Have you both gone mad?"

"We were watching Marlena go after another victim," Isabelle whispered in her ear.

Julia snorted. "Who is it this time?" Her gaze swept the floor and she saw with her own eyes. "Oh, my!" she giggled. "Kit will be furious."

James laughed. "Serves him right." His sister glared at him. "Well, now he'll know what it's like to watch your friend panting after your sister."

"He doesn't pant," she snapped.

"She's right," Isabelle interjected. "He doesn't pant, but he does fairly smolder when he looks at you."

Julia rolled her eyes. "You're not helping."

"Oh, I'd say she's helping just fine," James snorted. It rankled him to think of anybody, let alone one of his best friends, panting or smoldering in the direction of his baby sister.

"Oh, she's made her move," Julia whispered and held her breath.

James looked over at Parker but he was still standing alone. His eyes swept the floor and he noticed that Miss Barnes had positioned herself directly beside Anna. He was going to ask why when Isabelle answered.

"It's her signature move. Stand beside her prey and show the man that he has options. It's not about Parker, it's about winning against Anna to her."

He shook his head trying again to understand the way the female mind worked. And yet as he watched the performance play out in front of him, he had to question if men were truly smarter than their female counterpart.

The object of this trio's entertainment had noticed Parker looking her way briefly. Anna looked away briefly as somebody moved to stand beside her. She looked back and he was again looking at her. After being completely ignored by Parker for weeks, which was fine with Anna, why was he staring at her now? Parker took a deep breath and slowly started making his way towards her. And that's when Anna realized who was standing beside her.

"Hello, Anna," Marlena purred in such a charming tone. "Are you enjoying your season? I've been so busy dancing, it seems I don't have time to socialize at these events."

Anna nodded. "They can be quite tedious, but I am having a marvelous time."

"Of course, you are," she condescended. "Were you at the Lady Cordale's masquerade? It was such a wonderful time. And the men were so daring. Why Viscount Morely tried no less than three times to lure me out into the garden."

Anna felt herself growing ill. Was it all a game with Parker? He'd said as much to her that night. To see how far he could go without getting caught. And then Marlena went too far.

"At the unmasking, he told me he was so sorry for his earlier behavior but he just had to kiss me. But then I'm sure you must get the same drool lines as well." Marlena flashed her a dazzling smile.

Anna wanted to call her out right then, but then to do so, she would have to admit she was alone in the library with Parker at the time of the unmasking.

"Ladies," a voice appeared near them. Anna looked up to see Parker standing before her. Her heart skipped a beat, and she tried so hard to appear calm. "I was wondering, if I might have this dance?" he asked. She looked up and his eyes were locked to her own, waiting, pleading with her to forgive him.

"I should be delighted," Marlena purred and placed her hand in Parker's outstretched one.

Anna's face crumpled. Parker started at the hand in his for a brief second and then back to Anna. He shook his head and then pulled his hand back. "I'm sorry, miss," he murmured. "I meant Lady Anna. I believe my name is on her dance card for this number." He added that last bit to be polite.

Anna wanted to throw herself in his arms for his dismissal of the other girl's presence. He had just publicly declared his preference for her over the season's reigning beauty. She was so shocked that she didn't even think to protest as he led her to the dance floor.

He placed his hand lightly against her back and began to move her slowly around the ballroom. "I am terribly sorry for my behavior. Can you ever forgive me?" His voice was low and heady.

Anna lifted her chin defiantly. "That depends. Why are you sorry?"

Parker bit his lip. He knew this would be hard. Damn society and propriety. It was difficult to convey his thoughts properly while maintaining a stoic polite face. "I am sorry for everything. It was a mishap, and I was wrong to…" his words faded away. He could not tell her that he was only sorry for how he behaved after he knew her identity.

Anna stopped moving to the music. She swallowed. "A mishap? I'm a mishap? By all means, save your speech, my lord. You made your feelings on the matter quite clear weeks ago." She stepped away from him, but Parker held her hand to prevent her from leaving.

"Please, Anna," he whispered. "I feel low enough." The instant the words left his mouth, he realized it was the worst possible thing to say. Anna tugged her hand free and fled, leaving him standing alone in the middle of the dance floor.

He traced her path to the patio doors and outside. Ignoring the stares from the other party goers, he hurried after her. He had just stepped outside when he was grabbed and shoved against the side of the home.

"Care to explain why my sister just left you on the dance floor and fled in tears?" Kit growled.

"She's crying?" Parker asked in shock. Dear God, he had truly made a mess of things. He groaned at his own stupidity.

"Oh, stop it, Kit!" Anna snapped. "I was not crying."

Kit, hearing her voice, let go of Parker and turned to face her.

"Anna," Parker pleaded softly.

"Anna?" Kit snarled and turned back to Parker. "That is Lady Anna to you!"

"Kit, please," Anna begged and tugged on his arm. "You are attracting attention. I just want to go home. Can we please just leave now?"

Parker reached for Anna. "Please, I will call on you tomorrow to explain…"

"No," Kit clipped sharply. "You will stay the hell away from my sister."

"Kit, I just want to talk to her. You've got everything wrong."

Without another word, Kit draped his arm protectively around his sister and led her back inside where they collected Julia and then left. On the way home, Kit grew frustrated with Anna as she refused to answer any of his questions. Julia sat beside her friend, patting her hand for reassurance every time Kit raised his voice.

"Tell me what he's done, Anna." His voice was strained as he imagined the worst possible things in his mind.

Anna frowned at her brother. "Nothing, Kit. As usual, you have jumped to conclusions."

Kit snorted. "I have eyes as well as everybody else in attendance. Care to explain why you left Parker in mid dance?"

"I was tired of dancing," she answered sarcastically.

Kit shook his head. "I mean it, Anna. I want to know what in the hell that was all about. If he has said something inappropriate to you, I swear he will regret it."

"The only regret there will be is your own if you don't just forget it. I was tired of dancing, I walked away, and you have created something in your mind that doesn't exist."

Kit took a deep breath. His face was growing red, and he was about to lose his temper. "Anna, I will not allow you to talk to me..."

Julia reached over and squeezed her husband's hand. "You won't allow? For the love of God, she's not a child. I think you both need to calm down."

Kit opened his mouth but Julia gripped his hand tighter. He closed his mouth and then sighed. He pinned his gaze on his sister, who was now staring out the window ignoring him.

Once they arrived home, Anna made her way straight to her room ignoring Kit's demands for her to stop. He started up the stairs after her, when Julia grabbed his hand.

"Stop," she snapped. "She obviously doesn't want to talk right now, and you demanding that she submit to your orders will only infuriate her more. Give her some time."

Kit ran his hands through his dark brown hair. "I don't get it. What happened? He damn well better not be trifling with her, or I will kill him."

Julia wrapped her arms around him. "Don't think the worst. He could be completely innocent in all of this. A misunderstanding."

Kit blew out a long breath. "I just wish she would talk to me."

"She will," she whispered as she reached up to kiss his cheek. "She just needs time to calm down."

An hour later, Julia slid out from under her husband's arm and grabbed her robe. She tiptoed across the room to the connecting door leading to her own room, which she never used. Glancing back at Kit's sleeping form, she slipped out of the room.

She tapped lightly before opening Anna's door and gliding inside. Anna was sitting up in bed staring at her hands. "Spare me the details of why it took you so long," she said and rolled her eyes.

Julia giggled. She flopped on the bed beside Anna. "Alright, I won't. Let's have it. What happened?"

Anna took a deep breath and exhaled slowly. "I am such an idiot. I should have never let him know who I was."

Julia cocked her head to the side. Clearly, she was missing part of the story. "Start at the beginning, dear. I think there is a lot you've not told."

"The masked ball? The gentleman who stole a kiss?" At Julia's nod of recollection, Anna continued. "It was Parker. And it wasn't just a quick stolen kiss. It was passionate and exciting and anything but innocent, and much more."

"Oh, my," she whispered feigning shock. But she had already witnessed Parker staring at Anna earlier this evening and had begun to put two and two together. Then a devilish grin flashed. "Did you enjoy it? Was he as good as his reputation claims?" Anna blushed and nodded quickly. Julia squealed in delight. "Oh, that's famous! You never know if the rumors are true or not. Come on, spill it. I want to hear all the details!"

Anna shook her head. "It doesn't matter. When he discovered who I was, he was disgusted. He said it was a horrible mistake, and that he thought I was somebody else." She left out many of the details, because she was just too embarrassed to mention the rest.

Julia smoothed her friend's hair with her hand. "Oh, sweetie. Do you really think he meant that?"

"He called me a mishap tonight. A mishap! As if he hadn't insulted me enough already!" She swallowed the lump in her throat.

"Maybe he was just shocked to discover he was attracted to his friend's sister. It's some silly code of honor these men claim to hold dear."

"Kit didn't seem to let that stop him," Anna pointed out.

Julia smiled at the thought of the handsome man who had just made love to her. "No, he didn't. But he also has to put up with James throwing barbs at him every chance he gets."

"Please don't tell Kit," she begged again. "He would be so ashamed of me."

Julia hugged her. "Kit doesn't need to know." She hated keeping something from her new husband, but she also knew that he would overreact. She would keep her word as long as she could.

Chapter Five

The next morning as soon as it was acceptable to pay a call, Parker stood on the doorstep of the Ashworth townhouse. He knocked sharply and waited for the door to open. His knock was answered almost immediately, and he was shown inside. He took a step to follow Kit's butler, Nigel, but the butler informed him to wait in the entrance way. Parker frowned and had a bad feeling about this visit.

Kit appeared in the hall and looked at Parker. "Out," he snapped.

Parker was shocked at his tone. "Come on, Kit. I just want to apologize to her."

"Apologize for what?" Kit asked. Anna was still refusing to tell him what had transpired to make her leave Parker on the dance floor and run off outside. And even though Julia insisted she didn't know either, he wasn't quite certain his wife was being completely truthful with him.

Parker swallowed. He couldn't tell Kit everything or else he would find himself on the opposite end of a dueling field with his longtime friend. "I said something that I should not have said," he replied.

Kit raised an eyebrow. "And what did you say?"

"Please let me speak with her"

"No. Now, if you don't mind, I have things to do." He pointed towards the door and stared at him with a heated glare.

Parker sighed and shook his head. He turned around to leave but then stopped. "Will you at least tell her I am truly sorry?"

"Out," was Kit's response.

Feeling like an utter fool, Parker was left with no recourse but to leave without speaking to Anna.

The door had just closed when Julia walked down the stairs. "Was that Parker?" she asked.

Kit turned to look at his wife. "Yes. I threw him out."

"Oh!" Julia gasped. "Why would you do that?"

"He wanted to speak to Anna."

"And you now dictate whom she can and cannot speak to?" Julia commented.

"Please don't start. She still won't talk to me, and all he would say is that he wanted to apologize. I want to know what he is apologizing for."

Julia put her arm around him. She lifted herself up on her toes and kissed his lips softly trying to distract him from his thoughts. "I'm sure it is just a silly misunderstanding. I don't want to see you lose a friend over a wrong assumption."

Kit frowned at her. "You're trying to distract me from the issue at hand."

She smiled at him and kissed him again. "Is it working?"

Kit tried to give her a stern stare, but he couldn't help but accept her offerings. "Yes, it is, you little minx." He took her in his arms and kissed her long and deep to show her just how much she meant to him.

The next day Parker didn't even get to step a foot inside before Nigel informed him that the family was not at home to him. To him! Specifically, to him. Parker at least noted the butler's blush as he repeated the words of his employer.

The next morning, Nigel repeated his message before closing the door to him. The poor man looked ashamed to have to give the communication to his employer's longtime friend. Parker huffed at the humiliation of being barred from the home.

On the fourth morning, he brought a bouquet of flowers, but Nigel would not accept them to give to Lady Anna. When the door closed, Parker laid the flowers on the door step and walked away.

"He's persistent," Julia noted to her husband. He had opened the front door to run an errand and found the flowers. Rather than give them to their intended recipient, he threw them away.

Kit blew out a breath, his face red with anger. "This is beyond ridiculous. How thick is his head?"

Julia laid her hand on his arm. "Perhaps you should allow him in and find out what he wants."

"No," he clipped. "Not until I know what happened."

Julia laughed. "And how are you going to find out if you continue to ignore him?"

"She will tell me," he reasoned and left the house, slamming the door behind him.

"You can come out now," Julia said softly. She turned towards the rear door leading to the music room.

Anna stepped out of the shadows. "He was here again this morning?"

Julia sighed at sat down. "Yes, four days in a row. Each time he has been sent away." She motioned for Anna to sit down. "Anna, do you want to speak to him?"

Anna's eyes filled with tears. "Julia, I can't ever face him. If you had only heard how he talked to me. The things he accused me of doing. I just can't see him."

Julia reached over and hugged her sister in law. "Oh, dear. I'm sure he didn't mean what he said. People say irrational things when they are surprised. He was just shocked."

Anna shook her head. "No, I am pretty certain he meant everything he said."

The next morning and the next were a repeat. But the next morning, Julia happened to look out the window and saw a familiar figure standing in the park, watching the house. She shook her head. This had to stop. Anna wouldn't even leave the house for fear of running into him, and now Parker was holding her prisoner by spying on her from the park, as if daring her to leave.

Julia knew that Kit had gone out and probably wouldn't be back until later in the afternoon. She imagined Parker had waited until her husband had left before taking up his position. She shook her head. This had to stop. Calling for a footman, she crossed the street to confront Viscount Morely.

"What on earth do you think this will prove?" she demanded as she neared him. Her words faded slightly as she took in his appearance. He looked gaunt, almost sallow. His clothes did not appear impeccable as they normally did. But it was his blood shot eyes that gave her the most pause.

Parker looked up at her defeated. "I merely want to talk to her," he answered numbly.

"You are scaring her right now. Spying on her, intimidating her. Your mere presence is ensuring that she will not leave the house."

"I just feel so awful…" His words faded away. "Look, please let me talk to her."

Julia studied him and felt his desperation. She shook her head but answered in a sympathetic voice. "I'm sorry. Kit would be furious." His dejected expression fell even lower, so she added. "I could give her a message."

His head lifted hopefully. "Please tell her that I am very sorry and that I am an ass."

Julia's eyes widened at his vulgar speech but didn't comment. She nodded at him. He bit his lip as if wanting to say more, but finally shook his head and left the park. Julia watched him walk away and wondered what in the world had transpired between Anna and Parker.

Unknown to Julia and Parker, Anna was watching from the upstairs window. She wished Parker would leave her alone and stop trying to see her. Every time she thought of him, she recalled his harsh words to her and her humiliation at her own behavior.

But at night as she closed her eyes, the only thing she could remember was the feelings he had awakened in her. His touch, his kiss. The feel of his bare skin next to hers. How was it possible for one human being to make another feel so alive and so desperate for more?

A light knock on the door snapped her out of her day dreams. She moved away from the window and sat in a chair by the fire. "Come in," she called softly.

Julia entered slowly and crossed to the matching chair. "You've been up here all week," she noted. "Are you feeling alright?"

Anna smiled weakly at her. "I'm fine. I just don't want to get in your way, after all you and Kit deserve some time alone."

Julia reached a hand out and placed it on Anna's. "That's silly. This is your house, too. Besides, when you tell me that, you make me feel guilty."

"Oh, no! I didn't mean it that way," she quickly corrected. "I just, well..."

"I have a message for you," Julia said. When Anna's head snapped up, eyes wide in anticipation, Julia had a suspicion that Anna had watched her confrontation with Parker. "Viscount Morely wants me to tell you that he is sorry and that…"

Anna waited for her to finish but when she didn't she had to ask. "And?"

Julia sighed. "And that he is an ass."

Anna snorted. That was very true, but she could not comment or she might say more than she dared. Instead she nodded slowly, acknowledging that the message was delivered.

Jack sat across from the table watching Parker and smirked. For weeks now, Parker had rotated between drowning his sorrows and refusing to see anybody. When he was in his cups, Jack was amused at the tales of Parker the hero chastising the young lady from nearly ruining herself and throwing herself at the hero of Parker's story. But after several weeks of hearing this, Jack had finally had enough.

"You know, I think your problem isn't that you damn near made love to her or that she let herself be seduced by a professional, but that you enjoyed her up to that point of discovering her identity and you can't get the little darling out of your mind." He sat back in his chair and waited for Parker to react.

Parker lifted his head and glared at his friend. "You couldn't be more wrong," he growled. "Her behavior was atrocious, and you think I'm the bad guy?"

Jack leaned back in his chair and crossed his arms. "So tell me, Mr. Self-Righteousness. When you lay down at night and close your eyes, do you see the inside of your eyelids or does the image of her haunt you? Does it invade your dreams? Do you want to find out how the evening would have ended had she not been Kit's sister?" He flashed his wicked sly smirk at his friend and watched.

Parker shivered at Jack's words. Each and every one was the truth, but he would never admit it. And he could never act on it. He just needed a distraction to push the sight of Anna out of his mind.

"No," he clipped. "I sleep quite well at night." A lie! "She's just damn lucky it was me that night and not some other who would not have cared who she was. She needs to understand how careful she should be."

Jack snorted. "You can keep telling yourself that, but deep down inside, you know I'm right." He downed the last of his drink and pushed his chair back. "I'll see you around. Might stop and see Tessa."

Parker rolled his eyes. Jack changes mistresses on a whim. He never wanted one to grow too comfortable and even though they all knew his reputation, each one foolishly thought they would be the one to change Jack's fickle behavior.

"Morely!" a shrill voice shrieked from behind Parker as he roamed down the sidewalk. "Morely! A moment please."

Parker turned to find Jack's mistress Tessa bearing down on him. He cringed knowing what was coming next. "Mrs. Batson," he answered dryly. "How are you today?"

Tessa appeared out of breath as she approached him. "I would be much better if our dear friend Cavenaugh would come out of hiding," she answered through clenched teeth. "And just where has he been keeping himself?"

"Oh, well, I, um…"

"You men sure do cover for one another, don't you?" she snapped.

Parker suddenly sympathized with Jack. If Tessa was this demanding in public, he could only imagine how she berated his friend in private. "No, I have not seen Jack today, so I have no idea where he is keeping himself. If I see him, I will certainly let him know that you asked after him." He nodded and started to turn around.

Tessa grabbed his arm. Parker glanced down at her hand as if he couldn't believe she would dare do such a thing in so public a setting. "You may also tell him that I expect to see him this evening at eight o'clock or I may have to consider other offers."

Parker raised an eyebrow at her threat. Instead of replying, he reached for her hand and removed it from his arm. He was not a message boy, and he resented that she would give him such a directive. He turned back away from her and walked right into Anna. His hands shot out to grab her so she would not fall.

"Eight o'clock, Parker," the harpy called. "And don't forget or else I won't be very happy."

But Parker had already forgot about her. "Anna," he whispered breathlessly.

Anna's eyes were wide in shock, as were Isabelle's, who was standing beside her. They had watched the well-known mistress with her hands so intimately on Parker in utter disbelief. Her words echoed around inside Anna's head. Parker dared scold her for her behavior, yet his current behavior was beyond the pale.

"Anna?" he repeated praying that she would give him two minutes of her time. Instead she glanced up at him, sucked in a sharp breath, and tore herself away from him to flee. Parker recovered and tried to follow, but she rushed into her waiting carriage and the door was slammed just as he reached it. Parker could only watch while tears streamed down her cheeks as the driver pulled away.

He turned back around and cursed under his breath.

"What is wrong with you?" Isabelle demanded.

Parker's head snapped up. He had not even noticed his sister until now. "What are you doing here alone?" he asked.

Isabelle shook her head. "I wasn't alone until you managed to chase off my ride home."

He let out a heavy sigh and ran his fingers through his hair. "Come on. My carriage is over here." He took her arm and led her to the conveyance.

Once inside and moving along the street, Isabelle unleashed her anger on him. "What in the world is wrong with you, Parker? You flaunt that woman on the streets and then chase after Anna making her cry? Have you lost your mind?"

Parker stared at her trying to take in her accusations. "That woman?" And then he remembered Tessa. "She is nothing to me. She's mad at Jack and wants me to play the go between, and I am not getting involved in her drama."

"And Anna?"

"What about her?" he asked too quickly. When his sister shot him an exasperating stare, he was quickly reminded of his own mother chastising him for some infraction in his youth.

"What happened between the two of you?" she asked.

Parker turned away from his little sister, unable to lie directly to her face. He stared out the window and closed his eyes as Jack's words taunted him. Parker sighed and knew his friend was right. He wasn't mad at Anna for her behavior. He was mad at himself, because he could not get the memory of her out of his mind.

Isabelle leaned forward and covered his hand with her own. "Parker?" she called softly.

Taking a deep breath, he turned back to face her. "I hurt her," he confessed. "And I just want to tell her how very sorry I am, but she does not want to speak to me."

She nodded slowly and recalled Anna leaving her brother on the dance floor at the Yates ball. And then it hit her. "It was *you*!" she exclaimed sofly.

His blue eyes widened and he felt a sense of panic start to rise. "What do you mean?"

"The mystery man who kissed Anna at the masked ball," she countered and sat back and smiled at him smugly.

Parker returned her expression with a blank glare. He wasn't prepared to confess anything. Before he was forced to respond, the carriage stopped. He opened the door and jumped out, turning to take Isabelle's hand. "Run along inside and be a good girl," he grinned and kissed her cheek.

Isabelle stood her ground, hands on her hips. "Parker Heath Richards Albany! Don't you dare put me off!"

Parker tussled her hair and climbed back in the carriage. "I love you, little sister."

Isabelle was left standing there alone, shocked that he had just dumped her until she realized that their butler was holding the door open for her. She blew out a frustrating breath and stomped up the steps inside.

Anna arrived home and rushed inside, still crying her heart out. Unfortunately, Kit had just stepped in the hallway as she entered the home. She froze as she looked at him with tears streaming down her face but as he took a step towards her, she fled up the stairs.

"Anna!" Kit called and swore under his breath. He chased after her only to have her bedroom door slam right in his face. As his hand closed on the handle he heard the distinct sound of the lock turning. "Anna! Open this door!" he pounded on the door with his fist.

"Go away!" she screamed at him.

"I will not. Now open this damn door before I break it down!" he countered.

Julia stepped out of her room and stared at her husband. "What is going on out here?"

"I'm about to break this door down," he answered. He pushed on the handle and turned his body sideways.

Julia ran to him and grabbed his arm. "You are not!" she scolded. "You are going to walk away and let her have some peace."

"She's crying," he reasoned.

"And you bursting in on her, ignoring her wishes to be alone, will make her feel better?"

Kit stared at his wife in defeat. He locked both hands behind his head. "I just wish she would talk to me," he confessed softly. "She's been so sad, and I don't understand why. How can I make it right if she won't tell me what is wrong?"

Julia chuckled and led her away. "Kit, you can't force her to talk. That will only push her away more. You just need to give her some time and space to work through her own problems. She will talk when she is ready."

He sighed. "I swear, if Parker has something to do with her tears, I will kill him."

Anna was leaning against the door listening to their words. She tried to get her tears under control but the image of Parker with another woman devastated her. Try as she might, she could not forget the feelings he had raised in her in just a few stolen moments.

But worst of all was knowing that as she tried to get over her humiliation of experiencing something special with Parker, it meant absolutely nothing to him. She was just another woman to use. And to see him with that fast woman publicly making plans for an encounter later this evening, she realized that he saw her as the same type of woman.

She paced the floor trying to decide what to do. It was stressful enough hoping that Kit would not learn of her fall from grace, but she had a feeling that he was not going to let this go. She had to find a way to let this all blow over while she figured out how to avoid both Kit and Parker. After an hour of thinking and plotting, she knew what she had to do.

Julia was still trying to calm Kit. He was frustrated and knew that Anna was hiding something from him. While his wife droned on and on about letting Anna work it out herself and that he was over reacting and imaging the worse, he took a sip of scotch. He swirled the amber liquid around in the crystal glass and tried to come up with a way to make Anna talk to him. She had always been open and honest with him until this business with Parker had occurred.

"Kit, can I talk to you?"

Kit looked up to see his sister standing in the doorway. He jumped to his feet sloshing the scotch in his glass. He hurriedly set it down. "Please, Anna. Come in." He shot a triumphant look to his wife who was giving him one right back.

Anna shyly approached and sat in a chair across from him. Julia stood up. "Why don't I just see how soon dinner will be ready."

"You don't need to leave," Anna said.

Julia smiled at her. "I think you two need some time alone."

When Julia left, Kit sat down on the edge of his chair and looked at his sister in anticipation. "What's wrong, Anna?" he asked softly.

Anna looked down at her hands folded in her lap. "I would like to go visit Aunt Lottie for a while."

Kit tried to hide his surprise at Anna's revelation. He had expected her to say anything but this. "I see. You realize the season is just starting up. You've talked of nothing for years, and I would hate for you to miss it."

Anna could feel the tears coming to her eyes again. His words were true, but she would give it all up just to put some space between London and herself. "It's just been so stressful already. I don't think I am ready for all of it."

He sighed. He had never thought of a season as being stressful to a female, only to the men who hoped to avoid being trapped into a marriage by some title or fortune hunter. "I certainly don't expect you to make a match right away. Take all the time you need. There is no reason to get overworked with it all. Just relax and enjoy the balls." He gave her an encouraging smile.

"No," she answered shaking her head. "I have tried, and I just can't relax. It's too taxing. I need a break."

"Well, that's agreeable, but there's no reason for you to flee. I would certainly be pleased to stay home for a while, but if you tell my wife I said that I'll deny it," he grinned at her trying to coax a smile.

Anna chuckled despite her sadness. "No, I really just want to go to the country and get away from the hustle and bustle of town. I can't truly relax knowing that everything is happening just around the corner while I am hiding at home, afraid of it all."

Kit rose and stood beside her. He kissed the top of her head. "Very well. I will send a missive to Aunt Lottie on the morning. And if she is in residence and not galivanting around the countryside, I see no reason why a few weeks rest should be a problem."

"Oh, thank you, Kit! You are the best brother!"

He laughed and sat back down. Her crest fallen face had changed to one of hope now. He cocked his head and eyed her. "Anna? What happened with Parker?"

Anna's face suddenly became a blank canvas. "Nothing."

"Nothing?" he repeated. "That was a pretty quick answer."

Anna stood up. "I have nothing to say about Parker, and I wish you would stop making something out of nothing."

Kit realized he had gone too far. She had finally come to him, and he didn't want to push her completely away. "As you wish." He accepted the small victory and did not push for more.

Chapter Six

"Are you sure you'll be happy way out here in the country, dear?" Lady Charlotte Madden, dowager duchess of Cheshingham, asked her niece. "It's rather quiet and we don't have much social interaction."

Anna smiled weakly at the older lady. "That sounds perfect to me, Aunt Lottie."

The dowager studied her intently. "And what about the social whirl? You've waited a long time to make your bow only to run away from it after a few weeks? What happened to scare you off? Not that I am not pleased to have you visit."

"I just needed a break away from the stress of it all."

"Stress? Did you set your sights on a young man who fancied somebody else?" Lottie was never one to sugar coat anything. Besides, thanks to her well-placed sources, she already knew that there was a cause of tension between Anna and Kit's friend, Parker.

Anna glanced up at her aunt and wondered if she knew more than she was letting on. "Of course not," she answered. "I don't think I am quite ready for everything that is expected of a season."

"Hrumph," Lottie muttered under her breath. She knew there was a story hidden in the reason for Anna's sudden visit, but she also knew she would have plenty of time to dig up the truth. "Well, let's go see what Milly has prepared for our meal." She heaved her large frame out of a comfortable chair and reached for her cane.

Anna rose and rushed to rushed to take her arm, but Lottie slapped her hand away. Anna smiled. She enjoyed her aunt's company and had always admired her strength and grit. She obediently followed the dowager from the room and down the hall, knowing that whatever Milly, the cook, had prepared would be wonderful. Her aunt insisted on wonderful fare regardless of how many or who was present for a meal.

"And how is your brother's wife settling in to married life with that one?" Lottie asked just before she tasted her soup. She frowned for a second and then looked up at Anna for a response.

"Julia is getting along just fine. They are very much in love," she answered and wondered what had caused her aunt's frown.

"Is your soup too salty?"

Anna shook her head. "No, mine is delicious."

"Hmmm," she answered and took another taste. "And your brother? Does he spend his evenings at home with his wife or is he still galivanting about at his clubs and God only knows where else every night?"

Fighting back a snicker, Anna shook her head. "No, Aunt Lottie. Kit has been home every night when he hasn't been dutifully escorting myself and Julia to social events."

"Every night?" Lottie questioned a bit forcefully.

It always amazed Anna how Lottie seemed to know so much about the goings on in London when she never set foot there. Kit swore she had spies in every household, and it was a sense of amusement between the two siblings. "Well, he did go out briefly a few times."

"Ah-ha! I knew he would struggle to let go of his wilder ways." She flashed a triumphant grin. "I had hoped he would at least make a good show for a while."

"No! It's not like that at all," Anna said quickly defending her brother. "He's only gone out a few times looking for a friend. And he has returned home well before Julia or myself retired for the evening."

"And who would be so important that he would leave his wife and sister alone every evening?"

Anna sat up straight. She knew that he had been looking for Parker trying to find out what had happened between her and his friend. She lifted her chin and calmly answered, "I have no idea who he was looking for, Aunt Lottie."

The older woman pursed her lips together and stared at her niece until she noticed a slight blush form and the girl began to squirm. "I think you do know," she stated.

"Good evening," came a male voice breaking the tension in the room for the moment.

Lottie and Anna's heads turned to find Parker standing in the doorway. Anna gasped and stood up immediately readying herself to flee.

"Sit, girl," her aunt snapped. "Heavens, ladies do not stand when a gentleman enters the room. Perhaps your brother should have sent you to me years ago to teach you what is and isn't done."

The younger lady dropped back into her chair. She could feel her hands start to shake and her heart was beating so hard she knew the others could hear it. Why, why, why wouldn't Parker just leave her alone? He was the very reason she was hiding in the country, and now he had followed her here.

"Come in, my dear," Lottie instructed Parker. "I expected you two days ago."

Parker chuckled as he entered the room and kissed her wrinkled cheek. "I apologize for my delay. I was trying to tie up a few loose ends."

"Well, sit down and join us. Have you eaten yet?" She snapped her fingers at a footman who instantly appeared with a plate of food for the newcomer.

"Thank you," Parker said as he took a seat across from Anna. He glanced up at her, but she was staring at her own plate. He took a deep breath. "What have you ladies been scheming and plotting?" he teased trying to sound light hearted.

"I've been trying to drag out the latest gossip from my dear niece, but she doesn't seem to be schooled yet in that art. I shall have to work on that while she's here with me."

Parker nervously smiled at Anna, who was still looking down. "I thought all females enjoyed passing on the latest bit of news." He used the opportunity to study her. She looked beautiful in her green gown, but her face was very pale and he knew that he was the reason for her lack of coloring. Finding Lady Anna at his godmother's home had been as much of a surprise to him as he was certain his presence was to Anna.

"Wake up, gel!" Lottie snapped making both of her guests jump.

Anna's head snapped up and she was forced to look at Parker. His eyes silently pleaded with her to acknowledge him. She opened her mouth to speak but could not form any words. She felt a lump form in her throat, and she knew the tears were soon to follow.

The dowager could immediately sense the change in Anna, and despite her abrupt personality, she wasn't cruel. She reached over and lovingly covered her niece's hand. "My dear, you seem a bit tired. Perhaps you would like to turn in early tonight?"

Anna nodded and rose. Parker stood as well. She passed by him, never looking up, and swept out of the room, ignoring his pained gazed. When the door closed, he sighed and resumed his seat. When he looked back up at his godmother, he found her gaze piercing into his soul. He swallowed and looked down at his meal.

"I don't believe I've ever hosted a dinner party where the guests are more interested in what is on their plates than the company seated around the table," she noted. The scene that had just played out before her confirmed that once again, her sources were correct. Something had happened between her niece and her godson. "Let's have it," she snapped.

Parker's eyes slowly turned to Lottie. "I'm not sure what you mean." But his voice cracked as he spoke the words.

She raised an eyebrow at him. Tossing her linen napkin on the table, she placed both hands on the sturdy mahogany and pushed herself up. "I'm not a fool, young man. You and my niece have something that needs to be resolved. And it appears to me that you are the one who needs to be on your knees begging for forgiveness."

Parker rose to assist the elderly lady. "You are correct as always," he admitted.

Lottie patted his hand and smiled warmly at him. "Finish your meal, Parker. I think I will turn in myself."

Parker strolled into the library and went straight for the brandy. He poured himself a drink and circled the room, staring at the volumes of books lining the walls but not seeing any of them. He had tried to convince himself that he was angry with Anna for her behavior, but he knew that was far from the truth. How could he tell his friend's younger sister that he was fascinated by her. Taken. Obsessed. But Lady Anna was not the type of lady a man could trifle with and get away with it. To pursue her would be to open himself up to more than he was ready for.

He was only twenty-six years old, far too young in his mind to think about settling down. He couldn't understand why Kit had willingly fallen into that trap so quickly. Maybe when he was thirty he would start to think about marriage. But not now.

He drained his glass and reached for a cigar but then remembered Lottie detested the smell of smoke in her library. He grinned at the memory of the woman chasing men out of her favorite room in order to protect her beloved books. Holding the cheroot in his hand, he walked to the back of the house.

Stepping outside into the evening air, he struck a match and raised it to light the cigar. That's when he noticed the green silk dress. He dropped the match and took the cigar out of his mouth, shoving it in his jacket pocket.

Anna glanced up at him and sighed, but remained seated daintily on the bench. Their eyes met and neither spoke. Finally, Parker moved slowly towards her expecting her to bolt with each step he made. But to his surprise and delight, she remained seated.

When he stood directly in front of her, he decided to test her resolve and sat down beside her. They both sat in silence, looking out over the shadows covering the garden and listening to a fountain trickle water in the still night.

"I always enjoyed how peaceful it is here," he said softly. He waited to see if she would reply.

After several long moments, she replied. "That is one of the reasons I asked to visit Aunt Lottie. That and to be left alone."

Parker turned to look at her. "I didn't follow you." When Anna met his eyes, he continued. "Lottie is my godmother. She had written to me a couple weeks ago and asked me to help her with an issue she is having with a neighbor over land boundaries."

"Oh," Anna commented and was surprised that a part of her was disappointed that he hadn't followed her.

Again the silence grew between them. Parker didn't want to lose what had been his only opportunity to speak to her.

"Anna, I am truly sorry for the words I said to you. I was shocked, and I reacted very badly. I know I hurt you, and I will never forgive myself for that."

"That's what you're sorry for? For what you said?" she asked in disbelief.

Parker froze. He could do the honorable thing and tell her that he was sorry for what had transpired as he had done before, but he was defeated now. And he had no desire to lie to her. If truth be told, Jack was correct. He had enjoyed their experience together, and he had been angry because it seemed impossible for him to share such passion with his friend's sister. And so he sighed.

"Anna, I won't lie to you. I cannot in all honesty tell you that I am sorry for what we shared, because…Oh, hell. Because I was caught up in you and I quite enjoyed it." There. He had said it, and he waited for her to storm off, but she didn't.

"You aren't sorry for what we did?" she asked quietly.

"No," he answered emphatically. "Are you?" He turned to watch her face, to see her expression.

She bit her lip. "I am ashamed of my behavior and for what you must think of me."

Parker took her hand in his and looked at her long fingers. He caressed each knuckle as he searched for the right words. "Is that why you have been avoiding me?" When she tried to pull her hand back, he held it firmly in his.

"You saw me naked," she whispered. Her cheeks burned pink at that statement.

"You saw me naked," he returned.

She looked up at him with such a pitiful expression. "You touched me in ways that I didn't know were…" Her gaze lowered to her hand that he was still holding.

Parker raised his free hand to cup her cheek. "Anna, please don't be embarrassed. It was something special for both of us, and I would never tell tales about you over what was a private moment."

Anna nearly melted into his touch. Her eyes closed briefly, but then realized her mistake. She gave him a weak smile. "I thank you, Parker," she said quietly, his name a bare whisper on her lips. "I think I'll go inside now."

Parker stood and helped her to her feet. He continued to hold her hand as he gazed down on her pale face. "Please don't hide from me anymore. I do not think less of you for what happened. In fact, it is something that I will cherish for a very long time." He gave her a small smile for encouragement and waited until she returned the gesture.

He pulled her into an embrace. He stilled as he felt a sudden rush of the memory of their night together and how perfect she had felt in his arms, beneath his touch. He closed his eyes as he rested his head against her golden hair. "Oh, sweet Anna," he whispered so softly that she barely heard him clearly. When he finally released her, he smiled at her. "Goodnight," he stated.

Anna gave him a weak smile in return and stepped back. She nodded. "Goodnight, Parker," she answered and turned away to go inside. But even as she walked away, she could still hear his words clinging to her hair.

The next morning over breakfast, Anna was still pondering Parker's words and actions. He said he didn't regret what had happened, and he had enjoyed it. Then again, wasn't that what all rakes enjoyed, so perhaps it had been nothing more than a meaningless encounter. On the other hand, he had held her and whispered her name.

"Anna Ashworth!" her aunt snapped at her.

Anna drifted back to the present and looked at her aunt. "Yes, Auntie?" she asked.

"Hmmm. Are you going to tell me what has transpired between you and my godson that sent you running away from London?" Lottie asked with a heavy sigh.

"I don't know what you mean," Anna managed to say after a deafening pause.

Her aunt smiled knowingly at her. Lottie shook her head. "Don't give me that. You know exactly what I mean." Pushing her plate away, the older lady pinned Anna with a relentless stare. "I'm waiting."

There was no escape. Anna knew her aunt well enough to know that she would not give up. She sighed in defeat. "The Cordale Masked Ball. We didn't know who the other was and…"

Lottie's left eyebrow raised as she waited for further explanation. When Anna's eyes drifted towards the door, Lottie spoke up. "He's up and out of doors already. Won't be back for hours. So keep going, young lady."

"We shared a kiss," she whispered. "A simple kiss." She stared down at her hands folded in her lap.

"Hrumph," Lottie spat. "I can't even count the kisses I've experienced at a masked ball. That's no reason to run and hide."

"But he's one of Kit's best friends!" Anna cried, the feeling of guilt rising deep within her at how her brother would look at her if he only knew the truth.

Lottie snorted. "Nonsense. Do you think your brother felt a sense of honor to Kettering the first time he bedded his wife? I highly doubt it."

"Auntie!" Anna cried in alarm at the older woman's boldness.

Another snort. "Girl, I may be old, but I still have my memory. I know very well how passion can erase all sense of right and wrong in just the blink of an eye. I recall questioning my own morals afterwards. Do you think everybody doesn't know what happens in a marital bed? Polite society never speaks of it, but we all know."

Shaking her head to chase away her aunt's words, Anna let her mind drift back to that night. To the feelings and sensations Parker had awakened in her. How she would have never had the willpower to deny him anything. "It doesn't matter," she answered. "He's apologized, I've accepted, and that's done."

The dowager pushed away from the table and stood. "Except you can't get him out of your mind and running away will only keep those lingering questions at the forefront of your thoughts."

Chapter Seven

Parker checked his measurements for the sixth time that morning. He swore under his breath as he looked over the ancient property markers and the deed sent to the dowager by her new neighbor. Every time he had this figured out, his mind was filled with a beautiful lady spread before him, offering herself so willingly, and leaving him wanting her more and more.

The masked lady laughed at him in his thoughts. Taunted him, tempted him, teased him. Was this how the rest of his life was going to be? In his wild weeks with Jack, he had more women throw themselves at him than he could count, but not one had been worth his time. One had come close, but even as she led his drunken form into an upstairs room of the tavern they were in, he couldn't get the image of Anna out of his head. She had ruined him for all others, and Parker had left the bewildered bar maid before she could even close the door.

A heavy sigh crossed his lips. He knew he wanted her, but he also knew that she was forbidden fruit. Not only was she Kit's sister, but she was a young lady – one which a rake did not dally with unless he wished to find himself leg-shackled quicker than anything. She was just an obsession, he told himself. He would finish this project for Lottie, go back to London, and resume his way through the hordes of women who more than willing and safe to dally with.

But a little voice nagged at him that he was not going to forget her any time soon. Perhaps Anna had been correct in trying to avoid him. His mind had told him he had to see her alone again for the past few weeks, but when he had given her a simple embrace, his body had told him he wanted her. All of her. And that wasn't a possibility. He groaned at the endless circle he found himself in.

When he returned to the house later that afternoon, Lottie called to him from the library. He entered to find her cozied up before the fire with a book in her lap. "Did you get anything worked out?" she asked.

Parker smiled and sat down. "I was able to locate the old boundary markers, but I'm still puzzled as to why the deed markings differ so. I'll get it worked out."

"I'm not talking about the land," she tsked at him shaking her head. "Mercy, and I always thought you were one of the smarter ones!"

"Excuse me?" he asked, clearly confused at her set down.

"The girl! What did you work out about my niece?"

Parker swallowed. How had she known that Anna had consumed his thoughts so intently today that he had not been able to concentrate on the purpose of his visit. "What about her?"

Lottie laughed. "You two try very hard to play ignorant, but you can't hide the truth from me. I hear things, boy. Yes, even way out here. And I know you've been turned out of my nephew's home following an incident at a ball."

"She told you that?" he asked in disbelief.

A smile crossed her aged face. "Of course not. She denies I'm correct about anything, much like you are doing right now."

Parker stood up and walked to the opposite side of the room to the window. He inhaled sharply when he realized his mistake. Anna was sitting on a bench in the garden reading a book. His body tightened at the sight of her and his heart rate increased. He leaned forward and let his head rest against the cool glass.

"Are you going to tell me you aren't attracted to the chit? Because if you do, I'll call you a liar right this instant," she dared.

Parker lifted his head and turned back to face his godmother. "She's a lovely girl," he answered calmly.

"And?"

He snorted and walked away to examine the books on the shelves. "And nothing."

"I see," she replied. She stood up and walked straight toward him. "Then I won't call you a liar, but I will call you an idiot." With that she shoved her book into his stomach, and headed out of the room.

Parker grabbed the novel quickly before it fell and held it in his hands.

Four hours later, Lottie turned up her plotting over dinner by asking about Isabelle's season. "And does she have any prospects?"

Anna glanced up at Parker and watched his face pale. Parker shook his head. "No," he answered quietly.

"And why not? She's a dear, sweet girl. She would make somebody a fine wife."

Parker swallowed. He didn't like to discuss his sister's season. She wasn't fashionable, she wasn't sought after, she was quite happy being overlooked and out of place in London society. "Isabelle..." He couldn't find the right words to use. He loved his sister dearly, but even he could see the reason she did not have a single suitor.

"Isabelle is wonderful," Anna finished for him. "She is very well liked and is happy with herself. I think she is the best out there."

Parker looked up at Anna, thankful that she found such kind words to say about his sister. He knew they were friends, but he had never realized before what a champion Isabelle had in Anna.

"Posh!" Lottie retorted. "I think you've done a fair job of scaring off any young buck from calling on her."

"I have not!" Parker defended. "I would welcome any man in her life who holds her best interests at heart and who cherishes her for the jewel that she is."

"Any man, eh? What about Cavanaugh? I've heard he feels there is more to her than meets the eye."

Parker's eyes flared. "Jack better keep his damn thoughts to himself when it comes to Isabelle."

Lottie raised an eyebrow at his language but even she finally chuckled. "So not any man? What about young Chelmsworth? I've always thought Trey was the kindest of your lot. Had a lot of pressure put on him at a young age and has handled it quite well. And handsome to boot. Don't you think, Anna?"

Anna thought of her brother's friend, Trey and smiled. He was kind. "The earl is a very nice man, Auntie," she stated. "But I think he is too concerned about his sister's welfare and happiness to worry about his own."

"That would make him the perfect match for Isabelle. Parker, you wouldn't have any objections over that would you?"

Parker shook his head in confusion. "Well, I think Trey and Isabelle might have something to say about it. But still Trey is hardly the angel you two are making him out to be." He thought of his long-time friend, and while he certainly had a squeaky-clean reputation, Parker knew what Trey could get up to outside of society's eyes.

"Well, if Trey, of all people, is not good enough for Lady Isabelle, then is she to remain a spinster?"

"Of course not," he huffed. "I don't want her to marry somebody who would take advantage of her or hurt her. She deserves a husband who will love her and be good to her."

"Hmmm. I guess that's what every brother would want for his sister deep down no matter how much he thinks she is still a child."

Her words registered with both Parker and Anna at the same time. Her topic of conversation had nothing to do with Isabelle. Before either of them could respond, the dowager rose from the table and announced she was retiring for the evening.

Parker stood and both himself and Anna watched as Lottie made her way out of the room. When she was gone, he sat back down. His eyes met Anna's. "Would you like to go for a walk in the garden?" he asked in a hopeful tone. Anna nodded.

"I'd like to thank you for defending Isabelle," he said in a short tone. Anna's hand was tucked into the crook of his arm as they strolled along the garden path.

"I wasn't defending her. I was merely stating the truth," she returned.

Parker's other hand came up to cover her hand affectionately. "Still, it is comforting to know that she has friends who see her for who she is and not for..." he sighed unable to find the words to describe his sister.

Anna stopped walking and turned to face him. She looked up into his face and saw something close to pain looking back at her. "Parker, she truly is fine. She knows what people say about her. But she also has no desire to marry so soon. She doesn't want to go through the motions of pretending to be 'on the market' when her heart is not in it."

He stared down in disbelief at what he was hearing. "I don't understand. I thought young ladies lived for the chance to debut and find a husband."

She giggled. "You men are so silly at times, and yet we allow you to get away with your ridiculous notions." When his eyes narrowed in confusion, she added, "Why do men not marry at the same age as women? By that logic, you should have been married eight years ago."

Horror flitted over his face as the idea of marriage eight years earlier registered in his mind. "That's ridiculous!" he sputtered.

Her laughter filled the evening air like a bell. "No, it's not. If you were a lady, you would be considered hopeless at your age. Even past 'on the shelf' and already labeled a spinster, a burden on your family, a hopeless cause. Is that fair?"

"You don't want to marry either?" he asked, a bit shocked at her explanation.

She smiled. "I want to marry, but I don't have a deadline. Much as you said about your sister, I want to marry somebody who loves me, who will cherish me."

I would cherish you. He inhaled sharply and hoped he had not spoken the words aloud.

Her hand reached up and rested on his heart. "Let her have her time to find somebody who will hold her here above all others."

Parker's eyes drifted to her hand laying against his chest so intimately. Instinctively his own rose to cover it at the same moment their eyes met. He knew as clear as he knew his own name that he would never be the same until he had her completely. Mind, body, and soul.

The tension between the two was electrifying. Anna was suddenly transported back to their encounter that had started her on this downward spiral. To a moment when nothing else mattered except the two of them and the desire coursing through their veins. She leaned closer to him without realizing it.

His free hand snaked around behind her back, pulling her into him slowly. She raised her head to look at him and he was done. Her lips parted slightly, begging to be kissed, and Parker could not resist. Slowly he lowered his head to kiss her. His lips had just lightly brushed hers when there was a loud bang coming from the direction of the house.

"Careful, Mick!" the cook's voice scolded. "You could wake the dead with your clumsiness."

Parker raised his head and gazed down at Anna, her eyes now wide with mirth. He chuckled softly. "We're not out here alone," he whispered. Slowly he released her and stepped away. Anna managed to find the strength to stand on her own and also took a step backwards.

Reason returned to Parker as they stood together in silence. He fought the natural urge to ignore the servants and pull her back in his arms. But he knew he couldn't. He shouldn't have allowed himself to take her in his arms, but dammit she felt so perfect against him.

Anna swallowed. "We should go back inside," she stated quietly trying to hide the quiver in her tone.

He exhaled. "Of course." Taking her arm, they strolled back towards the house. When they reached the door, he held it open for her and bid her a good night, opting to stay outside alone for a little longer.

Anna made her way upstairs and into her room. She felt as if she were floating the entire distance. Parker might not have known who she was at the masked ball when he first kissed her, but he clearly knew her identity tonight. And still he had kissed her. Or at least started to until they were interrupted.

She crossed to her window and looked outside. Parker was still there, sitting on a bench staring out over the grounds. He shifted and leaned forward, resting his head in his hands for a few moments before standing up. When he turned around, his glance moved up to her window, and Anna felt herself shrinking backwards, embarrassed that she had been caught spying on him. Her heart skipped a beat knowing that he was still thinking of her as she rang for her maid to assist her for the night.

The next morning at breakfast, Parker gave Anna a warm smile as he joined her. He noted that Lottie was suspiciously alone. "And where is our host today?" he asked lightly.

Anna shook her head. "She is apparently breaking her fast in her rooms today, but she sends her apologies for her lack of courtesy to her guests." There was a hint of laughter in her tone as she spoke the words relayed just moments before by the butler.

"Ah. Well, I suppose I will have to suffer through with only your company this morning," he teased. Anna's head shot up to meet his eyes but relaxed when she saw the twinkling of good humor in his face.

"I agree with you, my lord. I will suffer as well, this morning." She tried to stifle a small giggle that bubbled forth from her. She coughed to cover it and asked casually, "And will you be back roaming the property boundaries today?"

He nodded. "I will. Going to the south lines today near the lake." And then before he realized what he was doing he added, "Would you like to go with me?"

Anna's eyes widened. Her mouth opened to answer but then closed again.

"Unless you have other plans," he said offering her a way to back out graciously.

"Oh, um, no I don't have any plans," she said softly.

Parker was shocked to find himself suddenly very pleased that she was going with him. "I'll see if Cook can prepare a basket and we'll have a picnic later."

"I'll just change and meet you outside," Anna answered.

Julia found Kit staring out the window of his study that morning. "Let me guess, you're missing Anna," she noted as she wrapped her arms around him from behind.

He sighed and turned around pulling his wife close to him. "The house just seems so empty without her, and I feel like I've failed her in some way." Kit rested his head against the top of Julia's. "Julia, do you have any idea why she's run off?"

"Oh, Kit. She hasn't run off. She's merely visiting your aunt," Julia assured him.

"Please tell me the truth, Julia. This is killing me."

Julia sighed. She had wanted to tell him several times to ease his own worry and to stop her husband from blaming himself, but she did not want to betray her friendship with Anna. Kit released her just enough to look her right in the eyes, and she saw the pain pleading with her.

"Oh, Kit. Let's sit down," she relented. Once they were seated on the sofa, she took his hands. "You have to promise to let me tell you everything without jumping to conclusions."

Kit sat up stiffly afraid of what she was getting at. "I don't know if I can do that."

"Then I guess you won't hear about it from me." She stood up and started to walk away when Kit grabbed her and pulled her back down.

"Agreed!" he ground out between clenched teeth.

Julia smiled. "The Cordale Masquerade. Anna was kissed by a gentleman." When Kit sharply inhaled, she patted his hand and gave him a stern look until he relaxed. "And when they removed their masks, they knew one another." She waited for her husband to put it together.

And he did very quickly. "I'll kill him!" he announced and stood up.

"Sit down!" she snapped.

Kit froze and glared down at her. "That bastard dared put his hands on my sister, and you expect me to sit down like it was nothing?"

"Sit!" she ordered. He did with a huff. "He had no clue who she was, the same as she had no idea who he was. And when he discovered that she was your sister, he laid into her. Called her behavior disgraceful, that you would be ashamed of her, and that she should know better. She was quite humiliated at his set down."

A slow smile crossed Kit's face. "He did? He scolded her that badly?"

She frowned at how pleased he was. "Yes, and he has been trying to apologize for his harshness ever since."

Kit fairly glowed with pride at his friend's reaction. "Well, it seems I owe him an apology when it appears he was behaving exactly as he should."

"You don't need to be so smug about it or are you forgetting that your sister was deeply hurt and embarrassed over the whole affair." Julia hated when her own brother acted so superior to her, and she was glad that Anna wasn't here to see Kit gloat.

Kit smiled and kissed his wife. "I think I need to go out for a bit."

Chapter Eight

Parker leaned against the two-hundred-year-old boundary marker and looked across the lake to the matching marker post high on a cliff he had marked the day before with a yellow flag. He looked again at the disputed deed and back up at the flag and shook his head.

"Did you solve it?" Anna asked from behind him.

He turned to look at her. She was holding a bouquet of wild flowers in her hand and looked so fresh and pretty that he forgot to breath.

"Well?"

"Oh," he mumbled. "No, I seem to be missing something here. The old markers line up perfectly with the original deeds but for some reason this new deed has the boundary line different."

She joined him, and all he could smell was her light perfume and the wild flowers drifting around her. "Where is the new boundary?" He walked over to a wooden stake set forty yards away.

"It lines up with the red flag up on that hill," he explained.

"What's in those caves?" she asked.

Parker's gaze lowered to the caves directly across the lake from where they stood. "The mines," he answered softly. "The mines!" He looked back down at the parchment in his hand and then back to the flags. "Anna, you are a genius!"

Anna laughed. "Well, I thank you, but for what do I deserve that title?"

"The mines! The old copper mines. Somebody is trying to claim the mines, and they've shifted the property boundaries just enough to include the entrances."

"Oh! Well, that's not very nice," she noted.

"I don't know why I didn't see this before," he stated. But he did know. He couldn't concentrate on anything with her so near him.

"Well, now that you have discovered the truth, we should celebrate with luncheon." She went back to the blanket and began to set out the fare Cook had prepared.

Parker joined her and poured two glasses of wine. They enjoyed their meal, laughing over Lottie's odd eccentricities but her kind-hearted devotion to those she loves. When the meal was finished, Parker set the basket aside and stretched out on the blanket. Anna sat daintily with her legs curled to one side.

"Are you going to take a nap now?" she teased.

"That sounds like a wonderful idea," he answered. "Care to join me?"

She raised an eyebrow at him. "I doubt that would be acceptable. Besides, I have my own personal morality officer who likes to lecture me on the do's and don'ts of proper behavior."

Parker rose to lean on an elbow and look at her. He had thought they had moved past that, but apparently, they had not. When she smiled at him, he realized she had been teasing. He laughed and she joined in with him.

With lightning speed, he reached up and pulled her down on top of him, her lips just a breath away from his own. Their laughter quickly disappeared as they each took in the others hungry stare. Parker lifted his head and met her lips.

Slowly, softly, he tasted her sweet kiss. Brushing his lips lightly along hers until he felt her relax and melt against his lean, hard body. His arms pressed lightly on her back, pulling her down against him. His tongue trailed the outer edges of her mouth, awakening her senses.

He shifted his body and rolled over on top of her, changing the tilt of his head to deepen the kiss. Her lips parted and his tongue slipped inside. She accepted him, her hand clinging to his back, the other drifting through his hair.

Parker had felt desire before but never such a deep pulling need. As if he were drowning, and she was the only one who could save him. He clung to her, savoring the feel of her breasts crushed against his chest, wishing this was her naked body pressed to him. She sighed softly, and he was brought back to the here and now. Of who she was and what he was doing. With one last soft kiss, he lifted his head.

Anna looked absolutely adorable, lips swollen, eyes heavy lidded, face flushed with passion. His mouth turned up in a boyish grin. "Lady Anna, you make me lose my head." Her expression changed quickly to one of disappointment. The back of his hand caressed her delicate cheek. "You are so beautiful, so perfect." He sighed. "What am I going to do with you?" He emphasized each word.

Anna shifted her hands to rest on his shoulders, and she gave him a weak smile not sure how to take his words. "Perhaps we should go back now," she said.

He nodded but did not move. Instead he studied her face, her complexion, her eyes, the tiny scar on her forehead. He memorized each detail wishing he had taken the time to do the same to her entire body when she was spread so glorious before him. He couldn't help himself when he pressed one more tender kiss to her full pink lips.

A shudder passed through Anna as he kissed her one last time. That kiss was not unplanned, was not reactive, it was decisive. He knew what he was doing and had no excuse for his actions except that he wanted to kiss her.

Parker took her hand and helped her to her feet. But he did not release her. Instead he pulled her into another embrace, her hands still locked in his hands but now behind her back. He kissed her again, slowly, lingering as he tasted her, tongues tangling together as if dancing a waltz. When he broke the kiss this time, he leaned down and rested his forehead against hers. "Oh, Anna," he whispered.

Kit walked into the gentleman's club and spied Jack sitting at a table with a couple of men. He grabbed a nearby chair and pushed it up to the table. Jack looked up at him and smiled through a pair of half drunken eyes.

"Southerby! Damn, have you grown bored with the little wife already?" he laughed.

Before Kit could reply, a terse reply came from across the table. "He better not be if he knows what's good for him. What in the hell are you doing here tonight?"

Kit glanced at the angry voice and saw James glowering at him. He chuckled. "No, I am more than content with my beautiful bride. As a matter of fact, she's the one who sent me here."

"Ah!" James laughed. "I wondered how long it would take her to tire of you. Find out you're not such a charmer, after all? Needed some breathing space?"

He snorted at his brother in law and ignored him. "Say, Jack. I've been looking for Parker for several days now. Any ideas where he's hiding?"

Jack leaned his head back and thought for a few moments. "Oh, yeah! Got a letter a while back from his godmother. She needed his help with some land dispute or something. He left a few days ago to help her sort it out. Said he shouldn't be gone more than a week or two."

Kit frowned. That would explain why he hadn't been able to find him anywhere. He signaled to a waiter for a drink. Julia had insisted he go out saying that she was just going to read and retire early, so he might as well enjoy some time with his friends. "Where's Trey?"

James nodded toward another table where Trey looked desperate to escape the older man who was talking to him. "Collinsworth has a daughter coming out this season. Appears he thinks young Trey would make him a fine son in law."

"Chelmsworth!" Jack bellowed. "Your deal! You in or not?" He looked around the table at his companions. "You fellows might worry about what old Collinsworth thinks of you, but I could care less."

Trey appeared and blew out a long breath. "Thanks, Jack. Thought I would never get away from him."

"Just so you know, I've seen the daughter. You'd best find you a list of excuses to avoid that one." Jack added as he slapped the deck of cards down in front of Trey.

James cringed. "Jesus, Jack. Keep your voice down. He could hear you."

Jack just grinned. "You don't think he knows his daughter's ugly as homemade sin? Why do you think he's in a club trying to pawn the chit off on unsuspecting men."

Kit choked back a laugh. He missed these nights, but he loved his evenings at home with his wife even more. Perhaps it would do him good to get out once in a while as Julia had suggested. Trey shuffled the cards and tossed them around the table. Kit smiled. It was good to be with friends. He would just wait until Parker returned to thank him.

Once again, Lottie excused herself early from dinner and left her two guests alone. Parker winked at Anna and she smiled shyly at him. "Would you care to go for a stroll in the gardens?" he asked.

Anna didn't respond right away. Once they had returned from their picnic, Parker had disappeared without a word until he entered the dining room.

"Please?"

She sighed and tossed her napkin on the table. "Very well."

They had walked a short way from the house when Parker stopped. "I wanted to talk to you, Anna."

Anna prepared herself for another lecture on her behavior and how this was wrong and how she should not have allowed him such liberties. She faced him with a grim expression determined that if he scolded her again she would give him a piece of her mind.

He pulled her to a bench and let her sit, but he remained standing, pacing before her. "I'm not really sure how to say this." He ran his fingers through his hair, turning his back to her. Suddenly he spun back towards her. "Ever since that night, I have not been able to get you out of my mind. At first I tried to blame you, but that was wrong. And I know it."

She didn't say a word. She couldn't possibly know where he was headed with this conversation, and so she waited.

"Anna, I struggle every time I see you. I want to hold you, to show you exactly how you make me feel. I can't touch you enough. You've bewitched me. I told you that I have no regrets about that night, but I do. I wish it had not stopped." He turned his back and walked a few steps away.

Silence settled between them. To say she was shocked was an understatement. She thought he might have feelings towards her, but not in her wildest dreams would she have imaged his confession.

"I know you are young, and aren't experienced with any of this. But I have to know if you felt anything. If you have a feeling that just won't go away. That leaves you wanting more. Not just a question, but a pure need."

He turned around and looked at her, his eyes pleading for an answer of some kind. She swallowed and then licked her lips, not know how inviting that simple gesture was to a desperate man. "I haven't been able to stop thinking of that night."

Suddenly he was on his knees at her side. "But in a good way? Or did you regret it?" He took her hands in his.

She felt his need for her answer, but she was so afraid of saying the wrong thing and pushing him away forever. She shook her head and noticed his eyes narrow in confusion. "I don't regret it now," she whispered. His face brightened.

"Anna, this is absolutely crazy and I know it. But I can't walk away from you. You are like a drug I'm addicted to. I need you." He looked down at that moment. "I would like to court you." He let out a long sigh and added, "With your brother's blessing, of course."

Anna giggled at his tone.

He rolled his eyes at her reaction. "It's not as funny as you might think."

"What about my blessing?" she teased.

Parker felt his cheeks grow warm, and then he smiled. "I'm sorry. I've never done this before. Would you allow me to court you?"

Her hand reached out to cradle his face as she studied him. "I would like nothing more," she whispered her answer. She leaned in and kissed him tenderly on his lips.

Kit settled down in bed with his wife nestled in his arms. She snuggled against him, sighing delightfully after their romantic interlude. He kissed the top of her head and chuckled. "Proud of yourself, are you?" he teased.

Julia giggled. "Me? Proud that I've turned one of the worst rakes in London into a stay at home pussy cat?"

He squeezed her lovingly. "Go to sleep, my dear," he commanded before reaching over to extinguish the lamp. He closed his eyes, contented as he had never imagined he could be.

And then it came to him. "That son of a bitch!" he bellowed and sat straight up in bed.

Julia jumped and looked at him. "What's wrong?"

Kit was already out of bed and reaching for his clothes. "Aunt Lottie is his damn godmother! That bastard has followed Anna. I'll kill him!"

Julia jumped up and grabbed his arm trying to prevent him from dressing. "Kit, stop! You can't go storming off in the middle of the night."

It took a good twenty minutes of arguing before she was able to convince Kit to wait until the morning. And when they returned to bed, it was merely a blank statement. Between Kit's huffing and muttered curses, and Julia's tossing and turning to ignore his complaints, neither slept.

Chapter Nine

Parker sat on the sofa in the small parlor, his arm resting along the back and one long leg stretched out the length of the piece of furniture. He smiled as Anna paced the floor back and forth before him. She was getting herself worked up and it amused him.

Suddenly she wheeled around and faced him. "What if we tell him that we've always adored one another. That's how he justified his wife to *her* brother."

He chuckled. "You want us to start off earning his trust by lying to him?"

She cocked her head and put her hands on her hips. "Do you have any brilliant ideas?"

"Come here," he said and held out his hand to her. She sighed and reached for him. Parker pulled her closer until he could pick her up and set her between his legs, his arms wrapped around her from behind. "That's much better," he said softly as he leaned back with her in his hold.

"This isn't at all proper, my lord," she scolded.

He nuzzled her neck with his lips. "I've told you, this is new to me. I'm not sure what is and what isn't proper."

Anna melted against his soft kisses. "Hmmm," she cooed and enjoyed his attention for a few moments. "But truly, we need to discuss this. What are we going to tell him?"

"The truth?"

Anna turned slightly and frowned. "And how do you think that would go over?"

He laughed. "It's rather warm in here. We should go outside and enjoy the beautiful day."

"I'll get freckles in that sun," she stated.

"You already have freckles," he teased.

Anna sat up and covered her cheeks. "I do not!"

"Not there," he said mischievously. His hand raised slowly and one finger brushed her left breast. "Right here is one. And there is another adorable one on the inside of your thigh."

She gasped and slapped his hand away. "Now that is absolutely improper!"

Parker pulled her back against him and laughed. "I'm sorry. I have much to learn, remember?"

"It seems that I have much to learn as well," a deep angry voice said behind them.

They both turned quickly and found Kit glaring at the scene in the parlor, his chest heaving.

"Kit!" Anna shrieked and jumped up from Parker's lap. "What on earth are you doing here?" She moved towards him nervously.

Kit didn't acknowledge his sister. His heated gaze was locked on his friend. Correction, his former friend. He couldn't speak. He wanted to kill Parker.

"I suppose you'll be wanting an explanation," Parker said. He wasn't looking forward to this, but he damn sure wasn't going to cower to Kit Ashworth. "Will you sit and hear me out?"

"No," he clipped. "Anna, pack your things. We are leaving this instant."

Anna stood her ground. "No, we are not, but you are welcome to leave."

Kit looked at his sister for the first time. "I beg your pardon?" he asked, stunned that she would argue with him.

"You heard me. You can either sit down and listen or you can leave."

His eyes narrowed first at his sister and then at Parker. "Like hell I will!" he bellowed. "I said go pack your things or I'll carry you out of here without!" He finally moved and stalked straight to Parker.

"Mercy! What is all the yelling about in here?" Lottie demanded as she stomped into the room.

"This is none of your concern, Aunt," Kit snapped back at her.

Before anybody knew what had happened, the dowager had crossed the room and grabbed hold of Kit's ear. "Don't you dare speak to me with that tone young man! I've put you over my knee more than once in your lifetime, and you're not too old to find yourself in that position again." She pulled him by the ear lobe towards a chair. "Sit!"

Parker couldn't help but smile at the ease in which she manhandled his friend. But he soon realized that was a mistake as his godmother released Kit and turned on him. Instinctively he took a step backwards.

"You, out!" she snapped.

The viscount didn't hesitate and quickly chose the path farthest away from the elderly lady and her deadly ear grip. He had reached the door when he heard her dismiss Anna in much the same way.

Once safely in the hall, he stared wide-eyed at Anna. "Care to take that walk outside now?" he asked.

She nodded quickly and the two made their way out of harm's way.

Lottie Madden pulled herself into her most regal duchess airs as she glided back and forth in front of him, her limp forgotten in her anger. "I know you are only acting out of a sense of duty to protect Anna from what you see as a threat, but I am telling you that you are overreacting."

"He's violated my trust, my friendship, and most importantly, my sister it seems," he growled.

"Oh, poohoo!" she charged. "And are you going to tell me that you went to your wedding with clean hands? That you had not compromised your bride in any manner?"

He opened his mouth to defend himself but then thought better.

"That's what I thought." She dropped down in a matching chair and leaned back, studying him intently. "Are you going to be so dense that you refuse to listen to them?"

Kit sighed. "I failed to protect her," he said softly.

Lottie chuckled. "You fool. You are failing to look at what is right before you. The chance for her to have happiness, a solid relationship with a man who is titled, well to do, and comes from a good family." Before he could interrupt her, she continued. "And just remember that when you point out every one of his faults, you are listing your own."

With a loud heave, Lottie left him to his own thoughts. Kit pondered what she had just said. He tried to overlook Parker's wilder reputation. It was no different than his own when he made up his mind that he was going to marry Julia. She stole his breath from him one evening, and he couldn't get her out of his mind no matter how hard he tried.

But with Parker, it was very difficult to see anything beyond...Well, the idea of any man looking at his sister that way turned his stomach and made him want to kill. Anna was such a good sister, such a good and smart girl. How could she think that Parker would be a good match for her?

"Can we talk now?" a voice asked from the doorway.

Kit turned his head to find Parker. Most men should be shaking and cowering for this encounter, but not Parker. He was standing as tall and straight as if he were going to question Kit about a horse race. His eyes narrowed at his friend's boldness. "I should just be done with it and kill you."

Parker snorted. "Taking the pious route, are we?" He sauntered into the room as if he had nothing to be ashamed of. "Will you listen or shall we round up our seconds?" When Kit pointed to the chair Lottie had vacated, Parker softly let out a breath.

He was nervous. No, he was actually quite terrified. He had never in his life approached a parent or guardian of a young lady, and here was somebody who would not only know every detail of his scandalous past, but who had also run the same gauntlet with him. There was no hiding who he was. Kit would not overlook his reputation to secure his sister a respectable title. This man would sooner kill him right now than give him any quarter.

"I won't lie to you," he started. "You may not like the truth, but that's the only way to come clean and ever have a chance of earning your trust again."

"You error in thinking that you had ever earned my trust," Kit snarled. "Start talking."

Parker sighed. "I didn't know who she was at the Cordale masquerade."

"And so you lured her away, like a lamb to slaughter." Kit jumped up from his seat. He could not sit still and listen to this dribble. "Cut to the chase. Did you compromise her?" He turned his back to Parker. "Could she be with child?"

"No!" he answered quickly. "No, she is not with child."

Kit spun on his heel. "Then how do you know about certain," he gritted his teeth barely able to say the words, "freckles?" The last word was spat out in disgust.

Parker cringed and closed his eyes. He had hoped that Kit hadn't heard that part of their earlier conversation. He shook his head and stood up. "Probably how you are imagining," he admitted. Before he knew what happened, Kit had him by the jacket and had slammed him against the wall.

"You bastard!" Kit pulled the other man right up into his face. He wanted to do great harm to his former friend. How dare Parker touch his sister! He released Parker and quickly planted his fist in Parker's face.

Parker recovered and shoved Kit backwards with a punch to the eye of his own. "It was wrong, but I didn't know who she was," he snarled.

Kit stumbled and caught his balance. He should have known Parker wouldn't stand there and take what he had coming. "That. Doesn't. Matter." His words were terse and clipped. He dove back at Parker and this time took him to the ground.

The two men rolled around on the floor, throwing punches, cursing the other. Furniture was overturned and the commotion could be heard throughout the house. But neither man cared. Until they found themselves dripping wet.

Parker landed a final blow as Kit turned his head to see how he had just ended up covered in water only to find Lottie's butler holding an empty bucket over the two men and his aunt glaring at them both.

"I will not tolerate such behavior in my home. If you're going to call him out, have done with it. But I warn you," she scolded sharply. "I shall be forever done with the victor, and I hate wearing black. You better decide right this instant, will I be planning a wedding or a funeral?"

Kit's face was red with anger. "A wedding will do for now, but I haven't ruled out the funeral afterwards," he said through gritted teeth.

Parker paled as Kit's words sunk in. Married. He was to be married now. His obsession with Anna was to become forever. He sighed. Had he really thought this would end any other way?

"Very well, I will got tell the bride," Lottie stated. She cast one glance at Kit and then to Parker before shaking her head and leaving the two men.

"Are you alright?" Parker asked in a low voice as he and Anna sat once again on the sofa in the same room where their worlds had been turned upside down by the appearance of Kit. Only this time, Lottie was dutifully present, chaperoning from the other side of the room.

Anna gave him a weak smile. "I'll be fine, but are you alright?" Her hand drifted up to his swollen and discolored eye.

He smiled like a proud school boy. "It's not my first." Parker reached for her hand and covered it with both of his. He wanted to reassure her that everything would be fine, that they would marry and live happily ever after, but he was terrified himself of that prospect.

"What happens now?" she whispered.

Parker took a deep breath. "Well, I've sent a message to my family, and your brother has notified his wife and a few others. Until they arrive, we wait." His thumb caressed the back of her hand as he spoke.

Anna struggled with the concept of getting married so quickly. Just a few days ago, she had agreed to allow him to court her, but now they were to be tied forever. Her future husband would be forced against his will to marry her. "I am sorry you are being forced…"

"Stop," he interrupted. "I am not being forced. We once agreed to put the past behind us and move forward. We will just do that again." He lifted her hand and placed a tender kiss on it.

Parker had already accepted that he should have spoken up weeks ago when he first compromised her. As time passed he realized that he wanted this marriage to take place. He had hoped to wait a few more years, but he had never before met a lady who made him even consider marriage.

Her heart raced. Could he truly not be angry at her or was he just trying to placate her feelings? She wanted so much for him to want her, and she had been so overjoyed when she thought he did. But now knowing he was given the choice of marriage or a duel, she wasn't so certain.

Parker put his arm around her and gave her an encouraging embrace. "We will be just fine."

"Ahem," Lottie cleared her throat and glanced over at the couple.

Parker removed his arm but leaned closer to Anna and whispered, "Now our chaperone turns up." He smiled at Anna who giggled in return.

Kit was hunched over a table in the library examining some papers when Jack found him. "You look awful," Jack noted as he tossed a folded paper down in front of Kit.

Kit unfolded the document and read it carefully before commenting. "Thank you for securing this," he said blandly.

Jack snorted. "Damn near gave the old bishop heart failure when I asked for it. Thought it was for me." He chuckled.

Even Kit had to laugh at that. "I expect we'll all need to be present when you request a special license to marry for yourself. The bishop wouldn't believe you otherwise."

"Why ask for my help and not your brother in law?" Jack asked even as he knew the answer.

"And have to deal with his gloating? No thank you. It will be bad enough when he and Julia arrive. But this is different."

Jack cocked his head and smiled. "How it that?"

Kit rolled his eyes. "Come on. This is Parker we're talking about. He's out for one thing. He just got caught."

"Are you certain?"

"Of course, I am." His tone was full of arrogance.

Jack smirked. "And what if I told you Parker was in love with Anna?"

An actual snort sounded from the marquess. "Why would you think that?"

"Because he's told me."

"I thought you just arrived?"

"I did," Jack answered. "I'm talking about weeks ago."

Kit placed his palms on the table and slowly rose. "You knew about this and yet you've never said a word?"

"Sit your judgmental ass down," he snapped in a rarely used but nevertheless effect dukish tone. "If you recall, you cried the same story to me over your beloved wife."

"That was different," Kit ground out.

Jack shrugged. "Quite right. It was different. You were obsessed with your intended. Sneaking around to catch a glimpse of her. Avoiding James like he had the plaque. Keeping me company. Imbibing too much until I was forced to give up my evenings to haul your drunk ass home, all the while muttering your undying love for the beautiful Julia Paget."

Kit snorted. "Not one of my prouder moments, but as I said, my situation was different."

"No, it wasn't." Jack corrected. "Parker behaved much the same as you did. Blubbering over the same fears, same concerns, same feelings. You just don't want to admit it."

"If what you say is true, why did you not tell me? For God's sake, that is my sister!" he snarled.

"Double déjà vu. James ripped into to me about the same thing, and I'll give you the same answer." His tone turned cold and hard. "Don't ever question my loyalty. Because it was my loyalty to Parker that kept me quiet. Had he not been so in love with the girl, I most certainly would have stepped in. But I knew that in the end, he would never dishonor her, just as you know."

With that said Jack casually walked out of the room and left Kit to consider what he had just said. It just seemed wrong. Jack Cavanaugh might be the worst hellion to run the gauntlet of scandals in all of England, but he was also true and loyal to a fault. He sighed.

The duke of Kettering was sitting alone in the parlor smiling over the strange way karma rears her head. Oh he had no doubt that Kit loved Julia, but to James Paget it was the way it had all gone down. And now Kit was getting his just desserts from Parker. It was a bit satisfying.

"Your grace?" a soft voice called.

James turned to find Anna, the blushing bride standing in the doorway. He stood and motioned for her to enter.

"I'm not disturbing you?" she asked.

James chuckled. "No, I'm just a member of the audience where as you are the starring role. Come, sit, please."

Anna nervously approached her friend's brother. She had known him most of her life, yet she suddenly realized this was wrong. She sat down across from him and looked down at her hands folded primly in her lap.

"What seems to be on your mind today?" he asked trying to hide the humor in his voice.

Her head snapped up. She had thought of this all night, and she was determined to do this. She took a deep breath. "Will you give me away at the wedding?"

"No." His answer was short and quick. Anna's eyes flew to his, shocked that he would be so terse. "That is not my place."

"But Kit won't even speak to me. He's being irrational. He's brooding and angry…"

"And he's being a brother," James replied. "Much as I was. But I can tell you this, despite my anger over the situation, I don't think I would ever get over Julia brushing me aside for such an honor as giving my sister in marriage."

"I see," she replied, her hopes dashed. "Well, I thank you for your time, your grace." She rose and had almost reached the door when he called out to her.

"Lady Anna, if your brother were not here, I would gladly do it. It would be one of my greatest honors, and it is still even to know that you asked. But I won't steal that same honor from Kit. He loves you too much."

Anna nodded, confused by his words. Surely if Kit loved her, he would at least speak to her instead of treating her as if she didn't even exist.

Chapter Ten

It took a full week before the required guests were able to arrive, the last being Parker's family. They were quiet, not sure what to expect. The message had only stated that Parker was marrying Lady Anna and to join them in all haste before it became his funeral.

"Mother," Parker said warmly. "I'm glad you were able to make it on such short notice."

"Well, this was quite a shock, although a pleasant one. I feared you would never settled down." She kissed his cheek and patted his back.

His father, however, was not so accepting. "I would like to discuss this with you, young man." He motioned for Parker to lead the way. Parker swallowed. His father could make any man cower, and he was not looking forward to this conversation.

Parker entered the library and stilled when he heard the door close behind him. "I take it this was not planned," the Earl of Tenworth started.

Parker turned slowly to face his father. Right to the point. No beating around the bush with his father. "It is a long story, Father."

"And you will tell me. Good God, Parker!" the older man barked. "She's one of your closest friend's sister, and a dear friend to your own sister. Have you no boundaries in your ways?"

"Father, it wasn't like that at all!" Suddenly he felt like a six-year-old child being called on the carpet for breaking a window. He blew out a calming breath and tried again. "The Cordale Masquerade. I did not know who she was."

Trenton Albany waited with an eerily quiet manner. Parker knew this tactic well. It was meant to unsettle him, to get him to say more than he meant to, and it nearly always worked.

Parker sighed. "Look, when I discovered who she was, I spoke harshly to her. I have been trying to apologize since, and when I ran into her here, we were able to talk. Kit discovered us alone, and you can imagine the rest."

"I believe you've left out quite a bit, Parker. Marriage is a long commitment."

"So is death," he muttered under his breath.

"Do you love her?" the earl asked of his son.

"No!" He answered quickly.

Trenton raised an eyebrow at his son's behavior. "A very quick response. Do you at least care for the girl? I can't fathom a son of mine being miserable or making his wife miserable."

Parker thought of Anna. He actually enjoyed her company. She was smart and witty and graceful, not a simpering fool who agreed with everything he said in the hopes of pleasing him. There was no doubt that he was physically attracted to her. She would be the perfect wife if he was in the market for a wife. But that point was beyond consideration now. He had two choices, wife or death.

"Ahem," the earl cleared his throat. "Did you forget the question?"

Slowly he raised his head remembering that his father was still present and had just asked him a question. "I had planned on courting her properly when I returned to London, but things took a slightly different turn," he confessed.

"So you do care for her? Perhaps you do love her, but you are just too stubborn to admit it."

Parker straightened at that accusation. "I don't want to hurt her. I compromised her, and I will do right by her." Even Parker heard the lie in his answer.

"Why now and not right away? It's rather disappointing that my own son would not step up the second he realized the line he had crossed." Trenton's gaze was piercing right into his son's soul.

"I had planned on it, but she ran away from me!" Parker returned.

The earl chuckled.

Parker stared in disbelief at his father not understanding where the humor was. "I spent weeks trying to get her to speak to me, chasing after her, and making myself look like a damn fool."

It amused the older man to know that the lady in question was not falling at Parker's feet as so many women did. This one would keep his son on his toes. Besides, he had seen young men wool gathering over a lady many times over in his lifetime. His son didn't realize how deep his feelings were toward his young bride, but Trenton Albany had a feeling Parker would soon find out.

Anna was sitting on her bed, trying to take in the fact that this would be her last night to sleep alone. After tomorrow morning, she and Parker would be husband and wife, and Anna was just now letting her nerves get the best of her.

Parker's mother had tried to give her a mother's reassurance to a young lady on the eve of her wedding given that Anna's mother was deceased. However it was an awkward conversation for Anna to have with the mother of the groom. No more than ten minutes after the countess had left, Julia had knocked.

Julia was less help than Parker's mother. Each time she tried to talk, Anna's sister in law would begin to blush and then sigh saying, "It's wonderful." After twenty minutes of this, Aunt Lottie arrived and shooed Julia out of the room.

Her aunt didn't hold anything back, much to Anna's shock. She had insisted that Parker would be gentle with her and not hurt her. Anna hadn't really expected that he would hurt her as she had already experienced firsthand just how Parker could make her feel. But she was curious now why everybody was warning her about pain.

After Lottie had left her to her own thoughts, Anna began to let her imagination run wild. She could still vividly remember the feelings and sensations Parker had stirred within her, and she couldn't understand what was so painful or what had she missed. She was still contemplating this when there was another knock on her door.

"It's open," she sighed wondering who was coming now. The door slowly opened and Anna gasped when she saw her brother standing there. She immediately blushed hoping that he wasn't here to give her a talk about what would happen tomorrow night.

His behavior didn't calm her fears. Kit was rather pale, except for the fading bruises from his tussle with Parker. He swallowed twice, trying to make his voice work.

"I've already been talked to by Aunt Lottie, Julia, and Lady Tenworth, so you need not share your wisdom with me," she blurted out.

He blinked at her, and then her words registered with him. "Oh, yes, well that's good." He walked closer and sat down on the bed. "I wanted to talk about everything that has happened." He pursed his lips together tightly. "I'm sorry for my outburst."

"It's alright," she replied hoping that he would just leave.

Kit shook his head. "No, it's not. I just want what is best for you." He ran his fingers through his hair. "I had hoped you would one day marry someday for love, like I was fortunate enough to do. I hate that you are being forced to marry somebody who will end up hurting you."

Anna laughed. "You are so hypocritical. What makes you think that I don't love Parker? And what makes you so certain that he will hurt me? Because of his reputation? I hate to be the one to break it to you, dear brother, but your reputation was much worse than Parker's."

Kit straightened at her words. "My reputation is not in question here. Parker has made it very clear that he does not want to marry…"

"He said he doesn't want to marry me?" she interrupted. Her heart sank. Had all of his words been lies? She knew he hadn't planned to marry this way; neither had she for that matter. But not at all? Not to her?

He waved his hands in front of his face. "No, no. He claims that he is quite willing to marry you. His only stipulation was that we wait until his family arrived. I meant that in the past he claimed that he would never marry until he was older and had to for an heir."

Anna let out a sigh of relief. "I know that already. But sometimes plans change."

"Yes, but this is Parker Albany we are discussing. He does not deserve you."

Anna stood up, fists clenched. "You know what I am tired of discussing? How you can only view me as your little sister and not as a woman. Because I am. We all are. Julie, Isabelle, Lucinda, and Sophronia! And you brothers better get used to the idea that we have feelings, thoughts, and identities other than being the sisters of some of the worst rakes in the country." She whirled around and walked to the window.

"Of course you have identities," he said after a long pause. "It's just that sometimes we know what men like us are thinking, and we want to protect you from that."

"Get out," she snapped. "I do not wish to talk to you anymore."

"Anna, please," he said softly.

She turned around with tears in her eyes. "I asked Kettering to give me away because you were acting like such a condescending ass, but he refused saying that would be too cruel even for you. Well, I don't care if a footman gives me away now. You have done everything you can to turn what should be the happiest day of my life into the worse."

She turned back to the window. "Now get out."

Kit shook his head and left the room in defeat. He headed downstairs to the library in desperate need of a drink.

The next morning Anna's room was filled with activity. Julia and Isabelle, Parker's mother, Anna's aunt, three maids all crammed into the room giggling and laughing, teasing telling tales of what was happening outside of the room.

"I walked by the library and happened to overhear Father giving the sternest of warnings to the groom and your brother," Isabelle giggled. Isabelle's father was well known to be a no-nonsense parent who didn't care what the rank of his brother's friends were. Even the dukes, Jack and James, feared his wrath.

"Hush," Maria Albany scolded. "You let your father deal with those two and you just concentrate on helping our beautiful bride."

When she was completely dressed, Anna was led to a mirror. She gasped at the reflection staring back at her. "Oh, my," she whispered.

"Oh, my, is right, Anna," Aunt Lottie said with tears in her eyes. "You look stunning. Your parents would be so proud."

Lady Tenworth put her arms on Anna's shoulders. "My son is a very lucky man, my dear."

Julie rushed forward. "Now! Let's see. We have borrowed and old covered, what about new and blue?"

"Well, the flowers are new, in a sense," Isabelle offered. "And your eyes are blue."

Aunt Lottie laughed. "We can do better than that. I'll be right back." She crossed to the room and opened the door to find Jack standing on the other side, his hand raised, ready to knock. "Your grace," she greeted.

"Who is it?" Anna asked still gazing at her reflection in the mirror.

"It's the duke," Isabelle answered.

Julia chuckled, "Which one?"

"The naughty one," Aunt Lottie answered with a disapproving scowl.

Jack actually blushed at her description. "Um, I was asked to deliver this." He shoved a small flat box at Lottie and fled.

Lottie walked over and handed it to Anna. "Open it up. Let's see what's inside."

Anna's hands shook as she carefully removed the lid. Inside was a stunning sapphire necklace and matching tear-drop earrings. "Oh!" she whispered. It was an exact copy of her paste set she had worn to the masked ball.

A chorus of gasps followed while she lifted the jewelry up. "There's a note," Isabelle said while picking up the paper that had floated to the floor. Anna unfolded the noted and read it.

The perfect jewels for my perfect Queen. Yours forever, Sir Lancelot

"What does it say?" Julie asked.

Anna closed the note and held it to her heart. A quiet smile flitted across her face, and for the first time in days, she felt truly happy.

"Well, that's your new and blue," Isabelle added. "Are you ready to do this?"

Her response was interrupted by another knock. This time it was Kit. One by one the other ladies excused themselves and left the room. Aunt Lottie shot Kit a warning glance. "We'll be waiting downstairs."

Kit closed the door behind them and looked at his little sister. He froze. His mouth opened and closed. He sucked in his bottom lip. "Anna, you look absolutely beautiful," he said softly. "I guess you are right. You are not a little girl anymore."

Anna blinked away tears. "Don't you dare make me cry, Christopher Ian Ashworth!" she scolded with a laugh.

He smiled. "I promise not to do anything to ruin your day." He walked toward her and took her hands. "Are you ready? Your groom has paced a hole in Aunt Lottie's parlor rug."

She looked up at him. "Is he upset?" she asked nervously.

Kit shook his head. "No. Just scared to death like most grooms are. Lord knows I was terrified the day I married Julia."

"You were? Why? You love her so much!"

He chuckled. "I was afraid she would back out. I was afraid I would forget her name during the vows. I was afraid I would be a failure as a husband. But most importantly, I was afraid that I wasn't good enough for her."

She took his hands as if to give him support. "I think you worried for nothing."

"Don't tell me you aren't the least bit nervous?"

Her smile faded and she looked in his eyes. "I'm terrified."

He led her over to a chair and sat her down. Kneeling down in front of her, he touched her chin. "Why are you terrified?"

She shook her head. "It just all happened so fast. And no man wants to be forced to marry his bride."

Kit sighed. "He's not being forced," he admitted though it pained him to say it. "He loves you and wants to marry you. He just doesn't know how to admit it."

Her eyes narrowed in confusion. "What do you mean?"

"According to Jack, he's been pining for you since the masquerade. Jack's version is a bit more amusing, but I'll save face for my future brother in law and not reveal what a love-sick fool he was."

Anna couldn't believe what he was saying. "Are you telling me that to make me feel better?"

He let out a long breath. "No, I'm not. No matter what my feelings are, the man loves you." She didn't respond but he thought she looked a little more at ease. "Now, let's go get you married."

Chapter Eleven

The wedding of Parker Trenton Albany, Viscount Morely, and Lady Anna Charlotte Ashworth, was quick and simple. The bride and groom spoke their vows quietly but clearly and when pronounced man and wife, the groom nervously gave his bride a tender kiss to the cheers and well wishes of those in attendance.

Anna remembered very little of the small wedding breakfast that followed. She did recall her brother whispering to her that he was only a messenger away should she ever need anything. The next thing she knew, she was being helped into a carriage and her husband sat down beside her.

The carriage pulled away from the house and Parker let his head fall back against the seat. "Well, that was fun," he said and let out a long breath of air. When Anna didn't comment, he rolled his eyes towards her direction. "Are you alright?"

"I'm fine," she answered quietly. She nervously straightened her skirt and folded her hands primly in her lap. "Where are we going?"

"Trey has a manor just a few miles away. It's much closer than my own estate," he explained. She didn't comment, and Parker sat back quietly for the remainder of the journey.

When the carriage pulled to a stop, Parker stepped out first and lifted Anna down. She glanced around at her surroundings. It was absolutely charming and she couldn't help but smile. "Like it?" he asked.

"It's beautiful. Does Trey ever spend any time here?"

"He and his sister spend a few weeks here every summer. Other than that, he doesn't come here very often."

She glanced up at the house. "I wonder why. If this were my home, I think I would spend most of my time here."

Parker cleared his throat and she cast an innocent look his way. "Are you finished stalling?" he grinned.

Her hand flew to her chest as if she were questioning if he was speaking to her.

The next thing she knew, Parker had picked her up in his arms and was carrying her up the steps. The front door opened and Trey's butler greeted them.

"Just direct me to our room, my good man," Parker said.

"Second door on the left, my lord," he said and stepped back.

Parker took the stairs two at a time. He found the room quickly and carried his bride inside. His foot kicked the door closed. When they were alone, he lowered his lips to hers and kissed her gently. He let her slip to the ground, never breaking the kiss, his arms still wrapped around her, holding her to him.

His tongue trailed along her perfect pink lips, tasting their softness. Probing little by little, she opened her mouth to him and he took the offering. Anna welcomed him, kissing him back, tasting, exploring. She sighed sweetly against his embrace.

Parker lifted his head and looked down at her. "God, I've wanted to do that for days," he said in a husky voice. "Damn, meddling family," he added with a grin.

Anna was suddenly nervous and shy around him. She gave him a weak smile.

He sensed her uneasiness, and released her gently. He strolled over to a table and poured two glasses of wine before returning to her and holding one out. When she accepted the offering, he smiled. "To us."

Anna sipped the wine while her eyes shifted nervously to the bed. Without realizing what she was doing, she took a step in the opposite direction.

Parker sighed. He took her hand and led her to an overstuffed chair in front of the fire. Taking her glass, he set both on the chair side table before he sat in the chair himself. "Come here," he said softly and pulled her down onto his lap.

Anna was stiff as a board on his legs, but he didn't comment about it. Instead he shifted her until she was reclined against him. "That's better, don't you think?" he stated. "I don't think I have told you just how absolutely beautiful you looked today." He handed the glass of wine back to her.

She took another sip. "Thank you," she returned. "You looked very handsome as well."

He fought back a chuckle. "Thank you." His fingers began to stroke her forearm hoping to ease her tension. "Would you like to hear something funny?"

Anna looked up at him and waited.

He smiled. "I took your findings to Lottie, about the mines. She gave me a sly smile and said she knew and the dispute had been settled months ago."

"I don't understand," Anna replied. "Why would she ask you to look into it?" And then it hit her. "She knew!"

Parker laughed and Anna's soft tones joined him.

"You know, Kit always believed that she had spies in our household. I think he was right!"

Parker noticed that Anna was no longer sitting so stiffly and was glad he had taken this route to ease her nerves. "Did you like your gift?"

"Oh!" she cried softly. "I'm so sorry. I completely forgot to thank you." She glanced down at the pendant resting just at the top of her breasts. "It is absolutely gorgeous. How on earth did you ever find one like this?"

This time he did chuckle. "I had it made. It was one of the things about that night that was ingrained forever in my mind."

She looked at him doubtfully. "You could not have possibly had this made in so short a time."

"Probably quite right. But the Duke of Brighton has much more pull than a mere viscount, and he was able to convince the right jeweler to complete it with all haste." He picked up the sapphire and held it in his hand. "Unfortunately, there are probably hordes of women in London right now wondering who Jack Cavanaugh bought such an important gift for and are just holding their breath to be the lucky recipient."

"Imagine the scandal if I let it be known that he purchased it for me," she teased. "I would be the envy of society."

He quirked an eyebrow at her and grinned. "Don't tell me you're one of his secret admirers, too?" He let go of her pendant and took her glass from her to return it to the table. He settled her closer to him, so that she was looking at him. She giggled.

His hand reached up to cup her cheek. "So beautiful," he whispered as her face rested against his palm. He leaned in and kissed her softly. He let his tongue trace the outline of her perfect pink lips taking his time so as to set her at ease. He carefully tested her resolve and probed his tongue between her lips once in a while until finally she opened to him and began to kiss him back.

Anna softened and leaned into his embrace. Parker's hands stroked along her arms and around to her back, delighting in the feel of her body. A soft moan left her throat and Parker deepened his kiss, tasting her, needing her, showing her how much he enjoyed her in his arms. His own manhood throbbed, but he knew that he had to take this slow.

Without a word, Parker stood with Anna cradled in his arms. He carried her to the large bed and let her slide down his muscular length until her feet touched the floor. With expert maneuvers, he went to work on the tiny buttons of her gown and let it slide from her into a pool of liquid silk at her feet. Her chemise was quickly pulled over her head leaving her in nothing but her slippers and stockings.

Parker lifted her in his arms and placed her in the center of the bed. A shiver ran down his spine. She looked so beautiful that he was almost afraid he would wake and find this all to be a dream. He quickly removed his jacket and cravat and then sat on the edge of the bed while he pulled off his boots.

His hands roamed along the length of her, caressing her, sending her promises of what was to come with a deep kiss. He raised his head and smiled down at her. He lifted her legs across his lap, discarding her dainty slippers and then slowly rolling her stockings down until she was left completely naked.

Anna knew she should feel embarrassed at her state of undress, but she kept telling herself Parker was her husband now. He stood and began to unbutton his linen shirt, discarding it behind him. She stared in awe at his broad, muscular chest sprinkled with blonde hair that trailed all the way down and disappeared beneath the waistband of his breeches.

As if he could read her thoughts, he unfastened his pants and pushed them down his slender hips revealing his manhood, standing proud. Her eyes locked onto the sight, and her heart began to race, her nerves coming back full force.

Once that was complete, he stretched out beside her. "That's much better," he stated before he lowered his mouth to her lips again and continued his exploration of her sweetness. Her hands moved to his shoulders and then, as she relaxed and returned his kisses with equal passion, her fingers clasped around his neck.

She pulled him closer to her, the memories of their fateful night rushing back into her mind. All of the feelings, the sensations, that he had ignited in her, that had been lying dormant for these past weeks, slowly rekindled and she wanted more. Her soft sigh played right into his hands.

He let his hands travel to her breast and cupped it to hold as an offering to his mouth. Parker's deft fingers worked her nipple into a tight bud. His tongue snaked out and flicked the peak for several seconds before he took her into his scorching mouth.

A small cry escaped her lips as his lips and tongue and teeth consumed her. Feelings of desire flooded her being and she clung to him, holding his head against her breast. Anna's breathing grew staggered as she tried to understand her body's response. She had felt this before, but the events that followed had dimmed these memories.

Parker's hands seemed to be everywhere. Sliding along her stomach, tracing the inside of her thighs, cupping her bottom, and then his fingers settled between her legs. They danced, they teased, they swirled and dipped bringing her closer to that escape she had been longing to experience again. When she was trembling at his touch and exploding in her passion, he let out a low growl and tore his lips away from her breasts.

Moving to kneel between her legs, he positioned his manhood. His gaze met her own. "I'm sorry, Anna," he said. "I cannot wait." He slowly pushed forward, closing his eyes against the tightness that met him. When he was stopped by her maidenhood, he stilled and looked at her again. "I'll try to be gentle," he gritted out.

Anna's eyes were wide in fear and anticipation, but she knew that only Parker could give her what her body so desperately needed. She nodded quickly. Parker took a deep breath and blew it out slowly to try to get his own body under control before he steadily moved forward and broke through her barrier.

She gasped and tears burned her eyes. He fell forward and kissed her lovingly, trying to take the pain away that he had just caused her. Little by little, he felt the tension leave her body. Suddenly his body revolted and he lost the last bit of control he had over it. He knew he couldn't stop himself now for anything. He moved once, twice within her and he was over the edge. His groan sounded almost painful as he spilled himself deep inside her.

When he opened his eyes, his face was buried into the crook of her neck. His body had finally stopped trembling, and he grasped that his entire weight was crushing down on her. And then he realized he must seem like an untried youth after his performance. He began to chuckle and then laugh before he rolled over and pulled her tightly against him.

Anna wanted to cry. Had she done something wrong? She couldn't believe he would make fun of her, but perhaps he thought she should know better what she was to do. "I'm sorry," she whispered.

"Sorry?" he asked between chuckles. "Why are you sorry?"

"Aren't you laughing at me?" she asked shyly.

He kissed the top of her head and laughed again. "No, I'm laughing at myself. I have dreamed about this night for so long, and when my dream finally comes true, I give the worst performance possible."

Anna lifted her head and looked at him. "I didn't do anything wrong?"

He smiled at her and caressed her flawless cheek. "No, my dear. You were absolutely perfect." His tone was no longer amused but low and serious. "I imagine after the next time, you will understand why I am laughing at myself."

"Next time?"

"Yes, next time I will make it perfect for you, even if it kills me," he promised.

Anna kissed him lightly on the lips and smiled down at him. "I thought it was perfect this time."

He chuckled and wrapped his arms around her. "Go to sleep now, Anna." She settled down in his arms and closed her eyes, amazed at how suddenly tired and sated her body was.

She didn't know how long she lay still with her eyes close, just enjoying the feel of Parker -her husband! – so strong and close to her. But she realized he must have thought she was asleep when he whispered against her hair, "I love you, Anna. And I promise to be the husband you deserve."

Anna smiled but didn't let on that she had heard him. She would let him tell her in his own time. She was content to know that he did love her. With that thought easing her mind, she drifted to sleep in the arms of the man she loved and knew that everything would be fine now.

The Duke's Mistake

Jared Ashton Cavanaugh, Jack to his close friends and the Duke of Brighton to the rest of society, has always lived as he wants. He loves women, gambling, drink, and raising hell and sees no reason to give up his wild life. But in the process of trying to thwart the only man who comes close the duke's rakish ways, he makes a mistake.

Jack playfully absconds a lady right from his rival's clutches and spends three days and nights with his prize at his country estate. But it soon becomes clear that this is an actual Lady, not to be trifled with in society's eyes or in the morals Jack's mother instilled in her son. However, she won't accept her fate, and Jack finds himself having to win a lady's heart for the first time in his life.

James, Parker, Trey, Jack, and Kit. Five of the most notorious rakes, scoundrels, and womanizers to ever wreak havoc on England. Men silently admire their daring, women secretly desire them, fathers despise them, and mothers are terrified of them. All titled, all wealthy, and all so devastatingly handsome and charming, they thrive on their reputations and scoff at social standards, taking what they want with nary a care for the destruction they leave in their path.

Fate would have them brought to their knees by the fact that they have sisters who will be entering society. Meeting men just like themselves who would think nothing of toying with a young lady's affections on a lark. They soon realize that in order to protect their sisters from their own kind, they must rein in their wicked ways and enter society.

But one by one this wild bunch finds themselves in the very situation they vowed to avoid at all costs.

About The Author

Allow me to introduce myself. I am Linda Kaye, a writer of historical romance novels and novellas.

As for my characters, I want them to be realistic. We all have flaws, and characters in a novel should as well. I want characters that come alive on my pages and stand out in your memory, even if they are not the type of person you would want to have as a friend!

Aside from writing I work full time and I am a mother of a son and a miniature dachshund. I enjoy reading (obviously!), genealogy, counted cross stitch, and watching football and baseball.

Some of my favorite authors and books are Harper Lee's "To Kill a Mockingbird", Laura Ingalls Wilder's "Little House Series", Johanna Lindsey, Kat Martin, and Eugenia Price

www.lindakayebooks.com

Made in the USA
Middletown, DE
07 October 2018